YANKEE TRADER

BEN TANNER—1799

YANKEE TRADER

BEN TANNER—1799

BY

Marjorie Chickering

FUNK & WAGNALLS
A Division of Reader's Digest Books, Inc.
NEW YORK

ACKNOWLEDGMENT

For their tremendous help to me in compiling the background for this book, I should like to express my warm thanks to Mrs. Bhima Sturtevant of Old Orchard, Maine—an authority on the social history of Maine; and to Mrs. Aurilla Gladding—Librarian at the St. Johnsbury, Vermont, Athenaeum.

To Rodney

Contents

AUTHOR'S NOTE

The reader may feel surprise that my last name and the name of the trader in this book are the same—Chickering. The facts are these: Late in the 1700's Luther Chickering and two brothers sailed from England to Boston, seeking freedom and independence in the rebellious Colonies. One brother drifted to New York State, the other stayed in Boston, but Luther made his way up the Connecticut River to the frontier town in the Green Mountains called Danville, Vermont. It was a town in name only, for there was no cluster of houses, no church or school, only small stumpy clearings among the huge trees and rutted trails leading to them and to grist and sawmills at the rapids of the brooks.

On a steep hillside above Sleeper's River, Luther built first a cabin and then a house of lumber, which he had helped saw at the mill. He married Betsy Balch of Lunenberg, and they raised a large family. Luther early saw the need for trade between the struggling new town and the established centers, and he started out as a drover. He collected cattle from far up toward Montreal and drove them to Boston or Portland, for in those days steaks went to market on foot. Farmers urged him to take along their potash, maple sugar, and other goods and trade them for tea, salt, tinware, and other essential things. Amaziah Barber opened the first store in the neighboring town of St. Johnsbury in 1799, and Luther's business expanded.

The hillside farm belonged to my husband's ancestors for several generations. Orville Chickering, great-grandson of Luther, married Alice Finley, great-granddaughter of Joseph Pope, who had settled on his farm in North Danville at about the time that Luther arrived to chop out his clearing two miles away. The young couple, grandparents of my husband, stayed on at Alice's home—the Pope place. The original hillside farm was sold and the Pope place then became known, and is still known today, as the Chickering farm.

YANKEE TRADER

BEN TANNER—1799

I

On the Trail

❖━━━❖C◦◦◦⊙◦◦◦O❖━━━❖

Ben Tanner stepped out onto the door stone and squinted in the early sun. Smoke from the cabin chimney floated straight up into the soft April sky, and down by the spring, he could hear Will singing off key as he filled Ma's water buckets. Ben threw a gunny sack over his shoulder and started down the path.

"Take care, son," cautioned his mother from the doorway.

Ben waved. Ma fretted whenever he left the yard. She couldn't seem to realize that he was old enough to take care of himself—or maybe she kept forgetting that this was 1799 and not the old days. As he skirted the clump of hemlocks, he could hear Pa's ax thudding, and then the swoosh of air as a big tree came down.

Ben watched a chipmunk scamper down Lord's Hill to the water. He remembered how Ma had been fearful of leaving Massachusetts—some of the women had been telling her how wild and dangerous it would be, living in Vermont—but Pa had eased her mind with tales of all the other settlers who were coming into St. Johnsbury by oxcart and flatboat.

Ben's thoughts kept pace with his long, loose-jointed strides as he followed the trail along the river bank. His hair was long and brown, tied at the back of his neck with a piece of rawhide, and his brown eyes were steady in a thin face tanned by March winds.

It was the kind of morning when it was good to be alive. He was glad Ma had wanted him to go clear to Barnet for the meal. She was hopeful that he could pick up some potatoes, too. It had been a long winter, and she was fretting because provisions were so low—not that they'd ever go hungry, Ben thought, as long as he had powder for his gun.

"Ben," Ma would say, "get your lazy shanks unwound and bring me a pair of rabbits. So much salt pork will be the death of little Goody."

Next to hunting, Ben liked to work with his hands.

"Always tinkering," Pa would complain. "You can think of too many reasons to keep you away from the woodpile." Pa had had a little more schooling than most farmers. He liked to read Shakespeare and those old Greeks. Ben sometimes wondered whether books had been good for Pa.

The trail left the river for a short way and climbed a steep knoll overhung with huge spruces. The sun never shone here, and grimy mounds of snow lay under the branches. Striding down to meet the swing of the river, Ben was jolted out of his musings by a dark shape on the far bank. A blunt snout lifted suspiciously, and a moment later a massive black bear went blundering off through the alders.

"Well, doggone," whispered Ben. "He's through hibernating, hungry as all get out, and ugly as sin. I'd better keep my eyes open now. And I don't want to meet Old Tattertail when I'm not carrying my gun."

Today Ben had left his gun at the cabin. The meal would be enough to lug home without adding the weight of a flintlock. Half a mile farther down the valley, Ben stopped briefly at a cabin to lend a hand to a little boy who was trying to keep a fire going under a sap kettle.

"Appears you've got your job cut out for you," Ben said. "Where's your pa?"

"Pa's sick abed with the fever," the child answered. "He's not here. He's to the Jewett's house in Peacham and Ma's with him."

"You all by yourself, then?"

"Jennett's here, but she's fixing to go to Barnet to bring back some seed and such. I have to keep this boiling till she gets back. Girls can't chop wood."

Ben thought that he'd seen a lot of girls who could chop wood. Still, it was a man's job. "Where's your woodpile, Johnny?" he asked.

"Name's Martin. Martin Peck." The youngster shook the winter's growth of hair out of his eyes. "I've got a pile of branches around the corner."

"I'm Ben Tanner. I'll fix you up so you can boil for a couple of hours."

The river, swelled by the spring run-off, lapped at the pile of limbs. Ben picked up half a dozen of the long, ungainly things—no use to drag them through the mud. As he turned toward the cabin, a sound of movement behind him brought to mind Old Tattertail, and he swung around sharply. The long tree limbs whooshed through the air.

"Hey, Jennett!" Martin shouted, but he was too late.

The branches caught his sister just above the waistline and propelled her swiftly and unwillingly straight into the icy waters of the Passumpsic.

Jennett screamed as she pitched forward, but she managed to save herself from falling full-length into the eddy of water. As Ben stood dumbly by, she straightened herself and stood dripping in a foot of water, rage written on her pretty face.

Her petticoats were soaked, and streams ran from the ends of her shawl. Ben got a glimpse of smooth, fair hair under her splashed bonnet, and of blue eyes blazing with anger. Finally, he came out of his horrified trance, flung the branches to the ground, and stretched out his hand to help her. For a second he thought she was going to refuse his help, but the weight of her skirts made independence impossible.

A few minutes later Ben was on his way down the trail, his face bright red. He was glad when he reached the mill on the river bank. The ponderous mill wheel creaked and rolled under the surge of green water moving briskly through the channel. He bargained with the miller for the sack of meal and was lucky enough to get a few potatoes, too.

"We sent most of our pelts to Portland by Luther. Made a real good trade," Ben reported. "Even got a book for Will."

"Your brother's a great lad for books," the miller said admiringly. "Take me, now—I never missed all that folderol, but I've certainly wished I'd learned more ciphering. My old woman thinks I ought to keep books on the business."

Ben didn't exactly share the man's admiration for Will, who was a year younger than Ben himself. If Will wasn't reading, he was thinking—doing his chores with a faraway look. He wouldn't hunt unless he had to, and nobody had ever been able to make him set a trap. Ben was kind of ashamed of him.

"Well," he said finally, "Will likes to study what those Greeks and all did two thousand years ago. Sometimes he reads some of it to us."

"They teach a lot of that stuff in the school they've just opened up over in Peacham. Once you're through the Caledonia County school, you can go right to Dartmouth or Yale if you've a mind to."

"Will's got his heart set on going to Peacham," Ben said, "but it costs dreadful dear. Six shillings a quarter, I hear."

"Ayah. A professor fellow from down-country is head of it. There's talk that girls can go, too, but I don't put much store in that."

Ben stuffed the gnarled little potatoes into his pack.

"Don't get lost," the miller shouted as Ben stomped off with his load. He grinned sourly. He couldn't get far enough out of town to get lost. How he'd like to go to Montreal or Boston or most any place new! Sometimes his longing to see the world was almost more than he could stand. He knew his restlessness often made him act mean at home and later he'd be sorry. But somehow he couldn't help this feeling of wanting to explore, to see new sights, to discover new things. If he could only get Luther Chickering to take him along—that would at least be something! Luther had started out as a drover, running the beef needed in Portland and Boston from the settled area around Montreal. Lately, though, there was so much produce changing hands that he had taken to trading goods, too. Luther followed the trails through the woods, going from small towns to hidden farms, and even hitting a big town on his trips. That would be the kind of life to lead!

If it wasn't for that scrawny Plin Edwards, Ben was sure that he might be traveling with Luther right now. Ben shifted his pack and frowned. Plin was a sharp-faced, shifty-eyed runt of an orphan who had been bound out to a merchant in Boston. The storekeeper had found himself unable to pay Luther for goods left on consignment and long since sold, and he had decided to have his indentured boy work out the debt.

It was just at the time when Ben thought he was finally going to be able to talk Ma into letting him go with Luther that the trader showed up with Plin. So it was Plin who plodded the rough roads, though Luther complained that he let the cattle stray, dropped packs into brooks, and did his chores with sullen carelessness. He whined at the loneliness, the walking, the bugs, and the solemn country people with whom they dealt.

Luther was often exasperated with him but kept him on,

for Plin had a few redeeming features. For one thing, he had
no more appetite than a chipmunk, and he always seemed
able to come by another tattered coat or shapeless pair of
shoes whenever the need was great, without asking his employer for money. So his upkeep was practically nothing.

For another thing, Plin could write a fine, legible hand.
Taught to read and write under the law that required all
bound children to be given this training, he was a considerable help to the trader in keeping accounts. Luther was a
sharp trader. He could estimate the value of a bundle of flax,
the weight of a hog, or the age of a tub of butter in nothing
flat—and never be proved wrong, either. People along his
route respected his ability and honesty and were glad to have
him make the long trek to market in their place. However,
he was no scholar and would sooner handle an ax than a quill,
so Plin stayed on.

During the winter, Ben had tangled with Plin at the smithy
over the matter of a swap of some personal belongings. Surly
and suspicious, Plin had sniffed at Ben's suggestion of the
terms of the swap. He'd managed to twist the conversation
around to make out that the unsuspecting Ben was a dolt.
Luther had laughed and told him to forget it, but Ben figured
despondently that the trader wasn't apt to sign on anybody
who couldn't manage a simple job of barter without being
made out a fool.

As Ben slogged along now under his load, he made out
Jennett coming toward him, holding her skirts above the
muddy path. As soon as she saw him, she dropped her head.
He thought she would pass without speaking, and that was a
silly way for the only two people within miles to act.

"See you got dried out," he said gruffly.

"Yes, thank you."

"I ran across an old he-bear this morning, poking around
the river," he ventured.

"Animals never bother me," said the girl coldly. She

walked on stiffly, and the color was hot in Ben's face again as he took up his load.

The sky had faded to gray in the east as Ben trudged into his own clearing. The candle flickered as he pushed through the cabin door and thumped down his load.

A little later, Ben scooped up the last of his pease porridge and turned his chair to the fire, grateful for the warmth and a full stomach. He could hear the thin piping of spring peepers in the marsh. Ben's father smoked thoughtfully, his pipe packed with a mixture of mullein and mint leaves. The flames tinted his full brown beard with red and flickered over the lines of his face.

Little Goody had drawn a stool near his knee and was braiding the yarn hair of her rag doll, her usually mischievous eyes intent on her work. Below her blue apron, the deerskin slippers that Ben had made showed their fringed edges. Ma didn't like them. She fretted that Ben was trying to turn her daughter into a savage, but Goody laughed. She thought the moccasins much nicer than the stiff shoes that the traveling cobbler pegged.

Will was hunched over a book, his elbows on the table and the candle drawn close. Ben's thoughts went back to the bear he had glimpsed. If he'd only taken his gun, that old bear wouldn't still be shuffling around.

His father cleared his throat. "Benjamin, Squire Hastings has sent word that they want help tomorrow repairing the Danville road."

"Ow-w!" Ben howled. "You mean I've got to shovel mud all day?"

"The road tax must be paid with labor by all able-bodied men and boys," his father said in his deliberate, rather formal manner of speaking. "However, to lighten your burden, let me point out that in part your duties will consist of driving the team of oxen."

Ben slumped dejectedly in his chair. He knew well enough that the roads were in bad shape, but he didn't have the faintest inclination to do anything about it. He wanted to get out and track down that bear.

II

Road Work

Ben didn't feel a bit more cooperative the next morning as he drove the slow oxen, yoked to the high-wheeled cart, along the curving road toward Sleeper's River. Other men, turned reluctantly from their own work, straggled down the narrow, muddy track with shovels across their shoulders and axes in their hands. Near the river, the group gathered to await instructions, the men making the most of their opportunity to swap talk.

"How's your wife, Barnabus?" Ben's father asked a heavy man with a pronounced limp.

"Better, Reuben. Much better."

"That's good news. I trust she'll be about in due course."

"Truth to tell," Barnabus Cole said wryly, "I'm looking forward to it myself. My daughter's cooking leaves much to be desired, and mine is worse. We hang the pot too high and the beans are underdone. Then we seem to set the spider too close and burn the meat."

Clopping hoofs turned their attention to a big man riding toward the group. "Here comes the big cheese," muttered Ben to Tim Ripley, a gangling redheaded boy.

"Horace Cutler, our esteemed Surveyor of Highways and Fence Viewer," Tim said in a whisper. The two boys snickered.

Cutler had a smooth-shaven, heavily jowled, amiable face. Though clad mainly in homespun, he still managed to create the effect of being dressed up. He wore a coat rather than the long, loose blue-and-white shirt preferred by most of the men. Many were bare-legged since they knew that the day's work would be dirty, but Cutler's stockings, below close-buckled breeches, were trim and light-colored. His horse pranced as he drew up with a shout of greeting.

"Glad to see all of you men ready and waiting," he roared genially. "We won't lose any time. As a key community for travel and communication, we must expand our facilities. I envision miles of well-drained roadbed over which post riders, drovers, merchants, and travelers will pass and repass."

Ben creaked off toward Brant's gravel pit with his slow-moving team. Cutler was setting men to work cleaning out ditches and chopping away bushes from the roadside.

Tim paced beside the cart. "If we're to surface a whole mile, we'll be at it all summer," he commented glumly.

"Aw, that's just some more of his big talk," Ben said. "All we have to give is four days' work, and that not all at once. We'll just fill in the mudholes, cut the sod out of the ditches, and crown up the middle a little."

Beyond them at the gravel pit, Barnabus grunted and swore softly as his bad leg slipped off a stone. The rest of the morning was spent in shoveling, making jerky trips to unload, and plodding back again. Finally, they fed the oxen in a sheltered twist of the road and settled down under an elm tree to eat. "Grass is getting good," Tim observed. "We were going to let the sheep out tomorrow. Now I don't know."

"Why not?" Ben asked idly.

"Bear signs all over the place. Last week Ma saw one right

in the clearing, nosing around the beehives. She beat on the
kettle and yelled and he lit out."

"By jingo!" exclaimed Ben, "I wonder if it could have been
the one I saw on the way to Barnet yesterday. Mean old
critter."

"Ma said he was a big one and pretty ragtag."

"Sounds like him. If it wasn't for this blasted road, I'd have
been in the woods today and chances are I would have got a
crack at him."

"We see a few bears every summer," Tim reminded him.
"Ma always has to shoo 'em out of our raspberry patch. All
you do is wave your apron at 'em, she says."

"Maybe so," Ben argued. "They don't usually come poking around buildings in daylight. But suppose this one's an
outlaw?"

"Um," Tim agreed, wiping his fingers on his breeches.
"Come on, let's get a drink."

They made their way down the steep bank to the river,
squatted, and dipped up the cold water with cupped hands.
Then Tim leaned back on the bank, his hands behind his
head. The bank was covered with the pale curled new leaves
of plants not long out from under a snowbank. Spring was
coming right along. Ben yawned and dropped down beside
Tim.

Suddenly he sat up with a start as an angry bellow sounded
from over his head.

"What's the meaning of this idle team? What are you lazy
scamps doing?"

Tim and Ben jumped to their feet and scrambled back
up the bank. "We just ate," Ben explained.

Horace Cutler's hearty smile was gone, and his florid face
was set in angry lines as he peered down from his sweating
horse.

"This will make a nice story for your fathers! Flouting
authority!"

"We didn't know we were behind time," Tim objected feebly.

"Your orders were to work your oxen, not dally by the river. Those orders are not to be disobeyed."

"We weren't disobeying," Ben objected. "All the men take time for a pipe after they eat."

"That's enough!" Cutler snapped. He yanked his horse around and rode off.

"Why, that two-faced windbag!" Ben sputtered furiously. "I don't see how the town lets him hold public office."

"Well, he does a lot for the town. He sure can talk. Most of the men don't want to take time out to travel around and write petitions to the General Assembly and all."

Throughout the long afternoon Ben yearned for the cool green of the woods. Pains were shooting up his back, his face was scarlet, and his hands were blistered. Finally, he jabbed his shovel into a heaped load, hung his hat on it, and prodded the tired oxen into the slow line of carts.

"I believe this is the last trip for today," Barnabus called as he limped beside his team.

When Ben topped the bend onto the Plain, he could see Cutler's black horse among the workmen, but before he had unloaded, the mounted man had disappeared. Ben looked a little anxiously at his father, but Reuben Tanner only greeted him gravely and suggested they start the pull up to their own place.

Ben was glad to see the cabin with its cobblestone chimney. The day had cooled off considerably, and Ma was taking in the washing. Ben had spent a good part of his evenings one winter whittling the clothespins she was tucking into her apron pocket. The clothesline was a strip of rawhide that he'd cut on the spiral from a whole oxhide.

Ben drove the oxen down to the narrow brook that swirled by the edge of the clearing and let them dip their great heads to the water.

"Bo, for gosh sakes, get a move on," he grumbled impatiently. "Jingo, you've drunk ten gallons already. I had a hard day, too."

The heavy yoke stood in the corner at last, the feed was forked in from the haystack, and he had the beasts settled. Ben splashed at the wash-bench outside the door; then he stepped inside where delicious smells were coming from a steaming kettle.

Ma had contrived a stew from some of the potatoes he had brought yesterday, a few withered carrots out of the root cellar, an unwary squirrel, and some early leeks out of the woods. There were even mugs of maple-flavored soft custard to end the meal.

The door stood open to the soft evening air, and Ben's father took his pipe to the wide door rock. When he was comfortable, Ben approached him cautiously.

"Pa, you heard how a bear scared the daylights out of Mrs. Ripley a few days ago?"

"Crispus told me of the occurrence today," his father replied.

"Recall how I spoke of one on the Barnet trail yesterday? Well, he was a mean one. I'm of the idea that it's the same bear. Pa, I'm bound I should make a swing around the hills tomorrow and see if I can cut his trail."

Reuben Tanner smoked reflectively.

Ben's brown eyes flashed in his lean face. "I bet it's an old outlaw and if something isn't done, he'll chew up half the young stock that's let out," he argued eagerly.

"Your concern is commendable," Mr. Tanner observed mildly. "However, if the bear is dangerous, destroying it would seem to be a task for a man—or better, a hunting party."

"But all the men are loaded with work. They don't want to go traipsing around in the woods, wasting time, especially now that this road job has got to be done. You know I've got a better eye in the woods than any of 'em. Look at all the pelts I took last year!"

"Probably true," agreed his father, "but the road work makes it impossible for you to go hunting tomorrow."

"You mean Cutler won't let me off?" Ben asked sourly.

"Of course you could put in your time later," his father observed, "but after today's incident, I'm inclined to think he might view your absence as slighting authority."

"Pa!" Ben burst out, jumping to his feet. "Tim and I didn't do one blessed thing! After we ate, we slid down the bank to get a drink, and he came up and jumped all over us."

Will stuck his head out of the doorway. "What's got you so excited?" he inquired in astonishment.

Ben glared at his slender brother. "So would you be excited if old Cutler bellowed at you and called you a lazy scamp."

Will looked worried—violence unsettled him. Ben turned away in disgust.

The morning after Ben was finally released from his enforced road work, he was in the woods before dawn. In his hand was his most prized possession, his rifle. He knew no other boy who owned one. One or two had muskets of their own—old smooth-bore blunderbusses—but most of them had to borrow their fathers' guns when they went out to hunt. Some of them made fun of the slender barrel, the small ball that Ben's gun fired, but when they saw what he could do with it, their eyes bugged out and they quit laughing.

Ben ran his hand over the slick maple stock. He'd been only fourteen that winter when he ran across the old Revolutionary War veteran in the woods. The man had been a Ranger through the war. After that, sick of seeing his wife and his little girl go cold and ragged, their teeth turning black from their wretched diet, and the mounting taxes of the new republic eating up their living in spite of never-ending work, he'd taken up his rifle again and marched with his western Massachusetts neighbors in the popular uprising that folks had named Shays' Rebellion after its leader, Daniel Shays.

Ben heard all this in hoarse, limping sentences as the old Ranger lay in the snow where he had fallen from exhaustion. He went on to tell how he'd left Massachusetts because of the warrant out for his arrest, officers not being included in the general pardon that Governor Bowdoin had issued to the defeated farmers, and the Vermonters had hidden him and the other stragglers.

That was in 1786, and Vermont was a country of rebels, well disposed to aid the fugitives. The old Hampshire Grants territory had been fighting unsuccessfully for years to become the fourteenth state and was still in danger of being swallowed up by New York. Vermont couldn't risk offending Massachusetts, so Governor Chittenden had issued a proclamation denouncing the rebel leaders and warning Vermonters against harboring them. But as one rebel to another, the Vermonters had welcomed the exhausted, despondent Massachusetts men.

Ben tried to leave to get help, but the broken man's nervous fingers clamped to his wrist and wouldn't let go. Ben could see it was too late anyway—the man was dying—so he huddled down in the snow and listened as the rough voice went weakly on. He'd thought to take up a little land and start again, the man said. But his wife and little Jenny had died of the smallpox, two days apart. That was years ago. After that he hadn't stayed anyplace for long. He coughed violently. Suddenly, looking at the sober-faced young hunter beside him, the man's eyes brightened a little. He motioned for Ben to give him a bullet. Ben held his breath, wondering, and handed one to him.

He asked Ben what his name was, and then, painfully, he

wrote something on a scrap of paper—only the rasp of his
breathing and the tiny crackle of the paper breaking the still-
ness of the winter woods. When he handed it back, Ben read
the wavering letters unbelievingly. *"My gun to Ben T.—L.
W."* He looked at the long gun leaning on a tree stump beside him. A rifle! He peered at the shattered man and was surprised to see a smile.

"Let me hold it," the dying man whispered.

Ben crouched beside him and put the gun and the paper
into his hands.

"Good gun," said the faint voice. His eyes closed. Ben
strained to see any movement. He put out his hand fearfully,
then scrambled to his feet and ran all the way home. He
wanted his father to take charge. And his father had. There
had been a flurry of surprise when the scratched note in the
dead man's hand had been found, but there was no question
about Ben's getting the gun. A well-loved weapon had been
passed on to an owner who now cherished it in turn.

It was still dark in the woods when Ben caught a shadow
of movement. A deer! His gun moved smoothly to his cheek,
his breathing stopped, and the ball flew—all in a second. Ben
ran, pulling out his knife as he went. At that close range he
couldn't miss. Quickly he carved out a section of haunch that
he could carry without too much trouble, tied it to a pole,
and slung it over his shoulder. With long strides, he moved
through the misty woods. The loaded pole had worn a gully
in Ben's shoulder by the time he slipped his burden to the
cabin table, but Ma was so happy that it was worth it.

After breakfast the next morning, Ben, Will, and Pa
tramped Indian file through the dead leaves, carrying some
old towcloth to wrap the rest of the meat in. The three of
them worked quickly to skin and quarter the deer. Ben noticed that Will took one look at the soft muzzle of the buck

and turned his head away. Well, Ben thought, would the squeamish ninny rather starve?

They divided the meat, leaving the less choice cuts behind. Ma couldn't use all of it very quickly, and it wouldn't keep in this weather.

III

Talk at the Smithy

When the meat was hung in the shed and Pa and Will had gone off to the woodlot, Ben stood rubbing his back against the corner of the shed. He cast a speculative eye at the brook. Way too early to think of taking a bath. Still, it had been quite a while since he'd had one. He felt hot and itchy.

With sudden decision, Ben started for the house. He'd risk lung fever and get cleaned up. The water would feel good. Then he'd clean his gun before he went out to the woodlot. Splitting rails didn't give him much call to hurry, anyhow.

Ben grinned at his mother, who was busily thumping her churn, and stepped through the cabin door. Spring sunshine streamed on the rough floor. A few dusty strings of dried apple and pumpkin still dangled from the rooftree. Ma would probably fly into her house-cleaning frenzy soon now. He picked out a towel from the chest and collected a handful of clean clothes and a blob of soft, gray soap. Reaching down his gun, he headed for the brook.

"You'll be in the woodlot, son?" his mother called, easing her back for a minute.

Ben turned briefly. "Not just yet. Be a little while." He didn't mention the bath and she hadn't noticed the clothes. She'd have a conniption over him going into the cold water. Ma looked hot and tired, too. She had plenty to do, like all the women. Good thing they didn't seem to mind it.

A few steps downstream, the brook curved around a knoll that hid the cabin, and a stand of uncut birches leaned over the water. In the sheltered place, Ben pulled off his shirt and enjoyed the feel of the sun on his bare shoulders. He tied back his hair tightly, thinking he ought to get Ma to whack it off again. He squatted on a smooth rock, dipped the soap into the icy water, and rubbed it up his arm. Goose pimples sprang up in rows all over his arms and legs. His courage just about gave out—and that made him mad. He shucked the rest of his clothes and lathered frantically, his muscles shuddering at the icy water.

Ben stuck his foot into the stream and watched his toes turn blue. What had he got himself into? Poised on the bank, he took a deep breath and willed his legs to jump. Just then a piercing shriek sounded through the trees.

"Ben! *Ben!*"

Ben's legs moved convulsively and he landed in the water with a gigantic splash. He came up sputtering, numb with shock, and scrambled dazedly out of the waist-deep water. What was going on? What possessed Ma to yell like that? She must be hurt.

Ben ran around the bend and skidded to a horrified stop. He leaped backward and doubled up behind a stump. Mrs. Johnson was dancing up and down beside Ma, her shawl fluttering and her eyes popping out.

"Heavens to Betsy!" exclaimed his mother. "Where can he be? *Ben.* Come quick!"

Ben cowered lower and turned his head to follow their staring gaze. Across the clearing a big black shape nosed among the beehives. Hens scudded squawking for the shed, dust and feathers flying. The big bear raised a heavy paw and knocked a beehive rolling. The women screamed in unison. Wet and trembling, Ben turned and raced for his clothes.

Buckskin stuck relentlessly to wet legs as he tried to haul on his breeches. Ben struggled harder and tripped himself into the dirt. Then the women came in sight, running toward the shed. Panic stricken, Ben rolled behind a rock and lay low, muttering awful imprecations on women who came to call, on breeches and on bears, as he tried to work his feet further into the tight buckskin.

That bear was the same one! Ben groaned and eyed his gun, leaning ready a scant ten feet away. The bear lumbered closer to the shed and sniffed inquiringly. Ben saw his mother plunge out of the shed with a heavy stick of wood in each hand. Awkwardly, she heaved one stick in the general direction of the black brute. It kicked up dirt a dozen feet away from the beast. Mrs. Johnson screeched again and dove into the shed. Ben looked hopefully toward his gun, but the woman's pale eyes still gleamed past the door post. He couldn't move yet.

"You get away from my bees, you dirty beast!" Ma screamed. She flailed her arms and let another missile fly. This one hit the bear's shoulder. He wagged his long head and shambled a few steps forward. Ben's heart almost stopped. Ma didn't know what she was doing. This bear wasn't one to be run off by a waving apron! He opened his mouth to yell a warning, but Ma made for the shed door and slammed it shut.

Blue and shaking, Ben squirmed on the grass and watched his shaggy enemy nose around the corner of the shed and pad across the front of the small building. Ben knew that the women were listening and squinting through a crack somewhere. It was good that other smells were attracting the bear's attention away from *him*. Ben held himself tensely quiet. Oh, what wouldn't he give for a shot at that thieving old animal.

The brute disappeared around the end of the shed and Ben waited tensely. Almost at once he came in sight, shambling deliberately back up the brook. He stopped to take a final swipe at an overturned beehive, then disappeared into the underbrush.

The shed door flew open and Ma and Mrs. Johnson fluttered out.

"If Ben had only been here," mourned his mother. They hurried into the house, and Ben began once more his war with the breeches. This time he wiggled in without trouble. The striped shirt felt good on his cold skin. Disgustedly he pulled on his shoes and snatched up the gun. He had only the charge with which the gun was loaded. His pouch and powder-horn were in the house. Ben hesitated. Ma wouldn't want him to set out alone. She'd make a fuss for fair if she knew what he was doing. One shot it would have to be.

He hurried up the brook, his rifle gripped tightly and his eyes looking all ways at once. Old Tattertail seemed to be taking his mangy carcass right toward the woodlot, and he must be traveling at a good clip, too. Ben trotted a little, his eyes intent on stirred-up leaf mold under the big maples.

Suddenly a shout rang through the trees. That was Pa! Ben lunged forward and in a minute burst out into the branch-cluttered clearing. He caught sight of Will crouching on top of a stump, his face white. The bear had halted and stood up, his dark bulk swaying uncertainly, huge claws protruding from his dangling forepaws.

Directly beyond him, Pa stood by the log he had been splitting, his ax gripped close to the heavy head. Then everything happened at once. Ben skidded to a stop and threw up his gun, the bear tumbled and dropped to all fours, and, with a powerful motion, Pa flung his ax. The honed blade struck a glancing blow on the bear's shoulder and dropped, leaving a spurting red gash. Will gave a strangled yell. The bear lunged sideways and Ben's shot whistled past, closer to his father than to the animal. As Ben clawed desperately for his knife, the brute whirled and galloped into the woods, smashing savagely through the underbrush.

Ben took after him, but the rough going slowed him more than it did the bear, so Ben quit fighting the brush and came back. Even if he'd had bullets for his rifle, it was doubtful if he could catch the beast now. That wound, though bloody, hadn't been deep enough to slow him down much.

Ben regarded his father with considerable respect. "Sorry I didn't peg him," he apologized. "Didn't figure on him dodging so spry, and you were kind of in my sights besides."

"I'm grateful that your marksmanship was as exact as possible," Mr. Tanner said dryly. "How came you to be so close on his heels?"

"He was at the house! That's the same one. He's been nosing around clearings all over. This time it was ours. He knocked over the beehives and sniffed around the shed. Ma and Mrs. Johnson shut themselves in there after Ma threw a stick at him." Ben suddenly turned scarlet. "I couldn't get to my gun," he said shortly.

Will took in the red face, wet hair, and clean shirt. "Were you in the creek?" he asked.

"Aye!" Ben admitted, and glared at his brother. He'd like to see that little softy dive into a brook in April. What if he should have been in the woodlot? Ma said cleanliness was next to Godliness, didn't she? Ben refused to listen to the small suggestion from his conscience that if he'd been more dutiful, he'd have been in the right spot when the bear showed up. He was disgusted and chagrined. Everything was working against him, and for the rest of the day he swung his ax in glum silence, meditating on his doleful luck.

The weather turned bitterly cold during the night. Shivering in his light shirt, Ben scrambled down the ladder the next morning and warmed himself before the fireplace. Blast the weather that couldn't make up its mind to be either winter or summer. **1385797**

Ma served him some steaming hot oatmeal that also helped to warm him. He recalled that Ma had never eaten oatmeal in her life until they moved to Vermont, where the many Scotsmen who had settled in Barnet and Ryegate twenty years earlier had introduced their national dish. Dubbed "horsefeed" by sarcastic Britishers, nevertheless it had grown popular among their Yankee neighbors and really come into its own in the famine winters. Splashing more maple syrup into his bowl, Ben reflected appreciatively that it made a smacking good dish.

When he finished eating, Ben bundled his cloak around him against the keen wind, tramped out to the shed, and picked up the shovel he had carved last winter. It had a T-piece on the handle and a broad, stout blade. Now all that needed to be done was to have the blade shod with iron. He put it under his arm and tramped down to Paddock's smithy.

Ben enjoyed the noise and smell of the smithy—sparks shooting from the clanging anvil, the reek of hot metal, farmers lounging by their quiet oxen. Huxham Paddock, swathed in a huge leather apron, was bent over the doubled foreleg of an ox, holding it against his bent knees and using a rasp on the ragged hoof. Over in the corner, one of his men was hammering out nails.

Ben finally noticed the boy sitting idly on an overturned bucket in a dim corner of the smithy. Plin Edwards. Anger and frustration boiled up inside Ben. There sat the reason why he couldn't get to see even a small part of the world.

Ben gave Plin a small nod. Often Plin was too sullen to talk to at all, and Ben hoped this would be one of the times. But when he stepped back after explaining his wants to the blacksmith and propped himself against the corner of a work-

bench to wait, Plin spoke. He gave Ben a twisted grin and remarked innocently, "Heard varmints have been making some
trouble around your place."

"Nope," Ben said briefly, trying to give the impression that
he wasn't a bit interested. How had Plin heard about it already!

"Well, that's funny," Plin observed in a perplexed tone
that Ben knew was pure humbug. "Way I got it, bear wandered in yesterday, tore up the beehives and chicken coop,
and scared the women half out of their shifts. Thought you
were a bear hunter, but seems the bears have to come hunting *you*."

Now the waiting men were listening. Ben seethed with
frustration. Just how much did Plin know about yesterday's
awkward situation? A knobby little runt like Plin had no
call to plague him about hunting, anyway. Why, Plin
couldn't tell a musket from a rifle, never mind shoot one!

"Reckon you wandered off on the wrong trail again," Ben
said pointedly. "Bear meandered into the yard, but only
tipped over a couple hives."

Plin's pointed face glowered at the remark about taking
the wrong trail, and Ben felt pleased with himself. City-bred,
Plin could never remember natural landmarks that showed
the forks on the rough roads. Ben couldn't remember ever
getting turned around, even in the deepest woods, but Plin
couldn't even follow the road.

"Pardon my forgetting you're a rip-roaring wonder with a
gun," Plin said sarcastically. "At least to hear you *tell* it."

Ben turned turkey red. He bunched his fists. "Want I
should say it in a way you'll *never* forget?" he threatened.

At that, Plin jumped to his feet and sent his bucket rolling.
"All the telling in creation won't make me believe it!" he
snarled, his black eyes spitting fire. "You and your big talk
and your big gun. You're so brave you walk right up to varmints and choke 'em to death—according to *you*. Now

you'd better change your story before somebody stuffs it down your gullet!"

"What makes you yammer so?" Ben yelled furiously. He was surprised that Plin hadn't taken to his heels. "What are you trying to get out?"

"You know full well. You were hiding in the grove while your mother drove off the bear with a stick! For all she begged you to grab your gun and down the critter, you stayed pinned to the spot until it was well away. Then you went tearing off pretending you were chasing it!"

"Why you . . ." Dumb with rage, Ben jumped at his tormenter, but Plin dodged like a weasel behind the workbench, and Ben nearly pitched onto his face.

"You keep your hands off me!" Plin sputtered. "Fighting won't change what happened. Your own brother told me how it was."

So Will made him out a coward. Just let him get his hands on that—that loudmouth. Ben charged headlong around the bench. Plin scrambled behind a newly hooped barrel and sent it whirling into Ben's path. Before Ben could recover his balance, an iron hand had clamped on his collar and hauled him up helplessly like a trout on a line.

"Now, my fine-feathered fighting cocks," boomed Huxham Paddock, his voice severe. "What's the use of such violence? Ben Tanner, you stand there!"

"You heard what Plin said," Ben choked, peering furiously out of the neck of his shirt.

"Aye. And why don't you yourself explain the happening?" Paddock released his grip, and Ben pulled his clothes into place. He eyed the interested men, some of them obviously enjoying the proceedings, and stood panting, frustrated beyond bearing.

"Well," prompted Paddock. "Were you hiding in the bushes or not?"

"I was not!" roared Ben. "I was taking a bath. And Ma had company!"

A snicker sounded from the doorway, then a guffaw that was picked up by the whole attentive circle and rose into a burst of raucous glee. Knowing the boy's pride in his shooting and how earnestly he hunted and trapped, it seemed irresistibly funny that he should be pinned down helplessly while game wandered about his own clearing.

Ben knew just what they were thinking. He stood for an instant in the face of the gale of laughter, then stalked grimly out of the door and away, his jaw set hard. Above the storm of indignation whirling in his head he heard one of them say, "Come now, lad . . ." He didn't pause. They'd acted just as he'd feared they would if the truth was let out. Let 'em laugh. There'd come a reckoning . . .

Ben stamped along toward home, planning horrible vengeance on Plin, on Will, on men with a perverted sense of humor. When he came in sight of the house, he saw Will in the shed, strewing bedding in the oxen's stalls. Ben strode in and spun his brother around with a heavy hand. Will's face was startled and perplexed, and a shade frightened.

"What possessed you to tell Plin Edwards that I was hiding from the bear?" Ben demanded. "Are you addled?"

"W-why, Ben," Will stuttered, backing away from his brother's angry glare. "I said nothing about hiding."

"That's not as I heard it down at the smithy. Nigh onto the whole town is laughing at me, and I don't relish it. Who else could have carried the tale?"

"Ben," Will said earnestly, "I spoke only of how it happened that you didn't shoot the beast."

"Yes, you spoke! When it would have been better if you'd kept quiet. How'd you come to be talking with that slithery runt anyhow?"

Will looked embarrassed and faintly sullen. "He's helping me with the advanced ciphering in the book Squire Arnold gave me. Plin's a figuring fool. I'll warrant he knows as much mathematics as the Town Clerk." His voice grew eager. "Know what he was doing last night? Casting out nine's. In every instance . . ."

Ben cut him short. He didn't want to hear any praises sung for Plin Edwards. "You should be ashamed to have dealings with an underhanded varmint like him. You can't trust his tongue. He'll make you the laughing stock of the town yet if you don't get shy of his clutches. You stay away from him, mark you!"

Will caught his breath as though argument was on the end of his tongue, but he only shook his thin shoulders and went back to his work. This had the effect of making Ben angrier than ever. Will just didn't seem to put any stock in his advice.

"What you so set on going to college for, anyhow?" he shouted angrily. "You've got learning on the brain!"

This didn't produce the proper result, either. Will just grinned. "Customary place for it, isn't it?"

"What good's it do to stuff your head full of folderol? Can't make you plow a decent furrow, can it?"

Will looked uncomfortable. In spite of the steady oxen, his plowing was terrible. "Squire Arnold told me education teaches folks to think," he retorted, "and that it's a means of improving our way of living. He said ignorance is at the root of superstition, bad manners, and uncooperativeness."

"My, don't we talk fine!" Ben jeered. "So you're practicing cooperating with Plin Edwards. Well, if that's what's needed to be smart, I'll stay ignorant. And *you* quit worrying about your way of living and keep watch on your tongue, you hear?"

Will was used to having Ben poke fun at him, and he didn't usually bother to argue. But now he thought of something more. "Oh, maybe you don't know," he said, "but your education is apt to get some jacking up, too. The Selectmen have voted a summer term of school. Starts the first Monday in June in Dr. Lord's great room."

"Did Pa say . . . ?" Ben asked anxiously, all his bluster forgotten.

"Yes, he thought the crops would be in by then, or most of them, and neither you nor I would be needed badly till haying time."

"That's not right," Ben said hotly. "They say I'm man enough to do road work, then they say I'm obliged to go to school like a child! I won't go!"

"You'll tell Pa so?" Will inquired with a touch of derision spoiling the mildness of his tone.

Ben turned and clumped out without answering. Heavily, he tramped out to the soggy cornfield and commenced heaving stones into position on the stone wall.

IV

The Schoolmaster

At dinner Ben's father confirmed his fears. With so little chance for schooling in the past, no opportunity was going to be passed up now.

"You're lucky to be sitting under a new teacher," Reuben Tanner admonished his son, who had never felt more unlucky in his life. "Horace Cutler has persuaded a young man just out of Dartmouth to teach the term. We were most fortunate to get him."

Sulking, Ben ate his Indian pudding without tasting it. He'd be pinned to a bench through the good summer days. Shut up with a gaggle of simpering girls while the woodchucks scampered unhindered through the garden and pigeon flocks wheeled overhead.

His disposition did not improve, and he moved through the days like a hanging thundercloud. His family took care to ask him no questions, and Ma brewed up a mess of thoroughwort tea and made him drink it. The bitter tonic nearly gave him lockjaw and did nothing for his disposition. He took no part in the talk about the coming school session.

When the first Monday in June arrived, Ben thought it

was more beautiful than any spring day had a right to be. He clumped morosely down the road, now smooth and dusty, and turned into the level stretch that led from Squire Arnold's house at the head of the Plain to Dr. Lord's on the bluff above the Passumpsic.

Will stepped quietly beside him, but Ben realized disgustedly, when he glanced at his brother's eager face, that his silence was of a different sort. Will clutched his thin stack of books carefully and carried a long lead stick. Pa thought these sticks wrote easier on the coarse brown school paper than quill pens did. He'd evened a crack between two of the kitchen floor boards with his knife and poured in the melted lead. Ben had snapped his stick into pieces and dumped them in his pocket.

Far down the flat ahead of them, Goody scampered blissfully toward school and friends, her petticoats swishing above bare feet. Ben twitched his shoulders under the new rough linen shirt. Nothing itchier in all creation than new towcloth. Imagine Ma going to the trouble of making a new shirt just to go to school in, and Pa perfectly willing to pay his half-cord of wood and six bushels of wheat as tuition for each of them! Ben reflected sourly that he would have a major hand in working up that wood payment.

"Golly, Will," he burst out, "how can you prance along as though you were going to a party? I'd rather be down with fever than cooped up in school all summer!"

"It won't be for long," Will murmured, "and any day that Pa needs us, we'll have to miss classes."

After a lifetime of carefully avoiding all unnecessary farm work, Ben now thought kindly of haying and harvesting. His eyes fell on the Hubbard girls hurrying up the bend, swinging a lunch basket between them.

"What are *they* doing?" he exclaimed. "They must be fourteen years old! And they live way over on the other side of Crow Hill."

"Maybe they want a chance to meet John Hammond," Will suggested.

"Oh, no! Is he the kind with a flowered waistcoat and a fancy shirt? I'll take the last teacher we had—Mistress Flint and her switch!"

Goody had joined a knot of little girls under the tamarack tree in the rough yard where Dr. Lord's inn stood. Here the occasional traveler, after laboring wearily up the steep pitch of the Barnet road, could put up for the night.

Ben squatted on his heels and scowled at the chattering youngsters. Tim eased across the yard and sat down beside him in silent sympathy.

"There's Barnabus Cole's little girl, Nancy," Tim said. "Barney finally got some help till his wife gets her strength back. Couldn't put up with his own cooking any longer, Nancy burned herself with a kettle of mush, and they were all out of stockings. So he rode to Barnet looking for somebody to take hold, and he came back with Jennett Peck. You ought to meet her."

"Umph," Ben said. Once was enough, he thought.

They sat and poked holes in the ground.

"Is Mr. Hammond scared to show himself?" Ben growled after a little while.

Almost on his words, a small bell sounded faintly in the open air, and the boys plodded across the yard to the door. Dr. Lord's big main room had been transformed into a proper schoolroom. Small girls and boys sat in the front row of benches, their legs swinging awkwardly short of the floor. The benches, hastily made of split logs supported by four spraddled legs, were placed around three sides of the room. Running before the back row of benches on each side of the room was a flat writing table made of a single plank and so high that many of the children would have to stand up to reach it. Beside the door was the teacher's desk, raised on a rough platform for a more commanding view of the room.

The new schoolmaster stood calmly by his desk. Ben shoved his way to a seat at the back of the room with the older group, and then took a good look at the new teacher. Mr. Hammond's fair hair fell back in waves from a smooth, untanned brow. His dark coat fitted neatly across his shoulders, which were, Ben noted, surprisingly broad for his short stature.

The master rapped sharply on the top of his desk with the handle of a knife, then laid it beside a stack of books. "Good morning," he said pleasantly. "I'm glad to see so many of you young men and women sitting in the lap of learning today."

One of the Hubbard girls giggled explosively, but he went on, undisturbed. "We will bow our heads for opening prayer."

The schoolmaster went about his business in a careful manner. He spoke first to his youngest students.

"What's your name?" he asked Ben's little sister.

"Goody Tanner," she whispered.

He gave her a small book. "Now then, can you read the first line? Tell me what it says."

Goody read stiffly, "I—see—a—bear."

Smothered laughs broke out among the older boys, and Ben felt the furtive glances in his direction. He glared around him until the snickers died away. The schoolmaster stared deliberately at the group, then turned back to Goody.

"Look carefully at the last word," he said. "The word is 'bird.' Write it twice for me." He passed on to the next small scholar.

"I see a bear," came a gleeful whisper.

Ben whipped his head around and glowered warningly right and left.

"I took a bath?" came the wicked whisper again.

Ben saw the quick glance that the gangling Hastings boy threw over his shoulder. Ben reached a long arm past Tim's head and shoved downward on a carefully bent neck. Abel Hastings tumbled to his knees, bumping the writing shelf and upsetting the inkhorn on Ira Sanger. Ira's sister screamed. Ira tried to scramble to his feet, but Tim's leg was in the way. One of the little girls twisted to see what was going on, fell off her bench, and began to cry. Most of the larger boys jumped to their feet.

The schoolmaster strode into the melee. Ben regarded him contemptuously. He didn't have a rod, so how did he think he was going to keep order?

"Who is responsible for this?" inquired Mr. Hammond.

Every head in the room turned toward Ben. Ben clamped his jaw and sat motionless while Mr. Hammond took two long steps forward. Suddenly Ben was raised firmly from his seat and steered rapidly across the room to the door, one arm being bent behind him in such a manner that he couldn't seem to do a thing about it. Blinking with amazement, he found himself standing before Dr. Lord's woodpile.

"Unfortunately, wood for the winter school term has not yet been donated," the schoolmaster said calmly. "However, Dr. Lord will no doubt allow us to work up some of his winter fuel. There is the ax. I will summon you at the end of half an hour."

Ben swung the ax viciously into a beech knot. Again and again he assaulted the tough stick until it lay in twisted slabs. How had Mr. Hammond lifted him out of his seat so easily? Ben muttered to himself in puzzled rage. What he ought to do was walk right on down the path and keep going. Maybe to the coast. Perhaps over in Portland they weren't so infernally bent on word puzzles and could use a man who knew his way around in the woods—one who could use an ax and an adz.

How he'd like to catch that Abel Hastings by himself after school. But Abel would stick with the others. Ben began to realize that until he shot that bear, he wouldn't get a minute's peace. If he could only meet up with the mangy old brute that was causing all his troubles, he vowed he'd be glad to take him on bare-handed. Then his shoulders sagged as he eyed the woodpile. He couldn't even go look for the bear. He was stuck with a white-faced quill-trimmer.

Just then the quill-trimmer stepped out and motioned to Ben. He made his way back to his seat in silence, noting with a small feeling of satisfaction that Abel was sitting on the floor beside the schoolmaster's desk, looking sullen and uncomfortable.

"I think all of you have been assigned except Benjamin," Mr. Hammond said briskly. "Now, I want all of you who are ciphering to the rule of four to come forward, but first Dyantha will collect the papers you have been working on."

During the week that followed, Ben found that Mr. Hammond, for all his careful speech and gentle manners, did keep order. The most reluctant students came to respect the master and, under the impact of his genuine love for learning, got down to serious study. Even Ben applied himself diligently, although part of that was due to his frantic haste to get through the reading book which he was obliged to share with the Hubbard girls.

The schoolmaster soon took a special interest in Will, lending him books in Latin and Greek and criticizing his penmanship endlessly. Will studied in the long summer twilight until Ma fretted that his eyes would give out. The candle supply was about done for and she hadn't had time for a dipping.

One evening as Ben came back from taking the cows down the lane, he saw that someone had joined Pa and Will on the door rock. As he drew closer to the dark cabin, he saw that it was Mr. Hammond. The schoolmaster's shirt was undone, and he hugged his knees in a comfortable, undignified way that surprised Ben.

"St. Johnsbury isn't a name that was brought up from the colonies like Windsor and Springfield," Mr. Hammond said thoughtfully as he leaned back on his elbows.

"I think Will's been talking about that lately," his father said, and lifted his shaggy eyebrows inquiringly as he turned to the younger boy. Will leaned forward eagerly. His thin face was outlined as his mother passed the open door with a candle.

"This town was named for St. John de Crevecoeur," Will explained. "He was the French Consul in New York at the time, and a great friend of Ethan Allen and Benjamin Franklin. Before that he served with Montcalm in Canada, and he spent a winter living with the Mohawks."

"M'sieur Michel Guillaume St. Jean de Crevecoeur," Mr. Hammond murmured. "I didn't realize. He was the son of the Marquis de Crevecoeur, but he called himself Hector St. John when he became a naturalized American."

"He explored the Great Lakes region and was adopted into the Oneida tribe," Will continued. Ben moved restlessly as he listened. He certainly was born too late. Imagine traveling around like that! And *he* couldn't even get out of town!

"I've read one of Mr. St. John's books," Mr. Hammond said. "They made a tremendous hit in England and France, and resulted in many people coming to the colonies."

"I wish I could get to read one," Will said wistfully.

"Have you been over to Danville?" Ben's father asked the schoolmaster.

"Not yet," Mr. Hammond said. "I hear it's a fine, growing community and the county seat."

"Danville was named after one of St. John's friends, the Duc d'Anville." Ben's father smoothed his beard reflectively. "It is indeed a growing town—and with growing pains. The halls of the courthouse resound at every session with arguments and arbitrations over boundary lines and grants. Many of the original settlers were squatters, and there's been no love lost between them and the grantees who came to their land later."

During their conversation, the strip of gray sky to the west had darkened until the pointed treetops could hardly be seen against it. Mr. Hammond raised himself easily to his feet. "I'll blunder off the road in the darkness if I'm not watchful," he observed, dusting at the seat of his breeches. "I think you'll enjoy that book, Will. Until next week, then. Good-by."

Ben propped his chin on his palm and watched the schoolmaster's blocky figure disappear into the dusk. He had never felt more fidgety. Somewhere ships scudded along under towering sails, carriages rumbled along glittering streets, soldiers marched, bands played. Ben groaned with frustration and stamped off to bed without a word.

V

Higher Education

———◆———

Ben woke the next morning in the same mood in which he had gone to bed, and for a few minutes he lay scowling at the rough rafters so close over his head. The small, open window at the peak of the roof showed a bright blue sky, and cheerful twitterings came from the young apple tree at the corner of the house. Will was still curled on his half of the cornhusk mattress, the quilt pulled up around his ears.

Will was always cold, and he got earaches when the wind blew on him. Sometimes he had no appetite. Ben scratched his bare chest and thought it must be terrible to be such a weakling. He sat up in bed and pulled on his shirt and breeches. Standing awkwardly so that he wouldn't bump his head, he tightened his belt, then skidded quickly down the ladder, jumping the last two rungs.

"Ben!" protested his mother as she swung the kettle over the flames. Ben padded out to the bucket and soused his head. He saw his father bringing the cows along the lane, his broad-brimmed hat flopping in time with his footsteps. Ben took the bucket to the brook and refilled it. He stepped back into the cabin and sank down morosely onto a stool to draw on his moccasins.

Goody was leaning drowsily against the table, still in her nightdress. "Got one foot in dreamland yet," her mother teased her as she moved the little girl gently out of the way. "My stars, Ben, do something about your hair. It looks like a hoorah's nest."

It was Saturday, and Ma decided she needed some things from the store. After breakfast, Ben tucked a package of butter securely under his arm and set out happily. On the Plain, he passed a pile of new lumber and guessed it was true what he'd heard about Andrew Dole and Lettice Barber getting her father's consent. When the new house was ready, there'd be a wedding. He crossed the low porch that Amaziah Barber had built onto his house when he set up the store and then stepped into the dim room beyond.

Amaziah was behind the rough counter, a heavy apron sagging from his angular shoulders. His nose was pointed, his chin pointed, and his graying hair stuck up in peaks. Sharp eyes regarded Ben from under steep-angled eyebrows. Ben wondered how he dried his face without tearing the towel.

He eyed the shelves behind the storekeeper. They were scattered with small packages, mostly wrapped in brown paper. In the corner were other and bigger piles of produce which had been brought in for trade. Wooden pails of maple sugar, wheels of cheese, sacks of grain, pelts, and potash stood ready for Luther's next trip.

Times when Amaziah concluded a cash sale were few and far between. Sometimes he forgot the price of his goods in shillings and pence, but he could strike a bargain in trade with precision.

"What's your wish today?" Amaziah questioned in his abrupt voice.

"Turnip seed mostly," Ben told him, setting his packet of butter on the counter.

"No seed," Amaziah said. "Not much of anything till Luther gets back. Been a long winter and a busy one."

"Too bad," Ben answered. "Ma will be provoked about that. Well, anyhow, she'd like a package of indigo for the dye pot and sixpence worth of tea."

Amaziah made careful notes in a leather-covered ledger and set the items before Ben. "Letty," he called through the rear door.

His daughter Lettice, sharp-nosed and unsmiling, came quickly to his side.

"Put this butter into the last tub," he directed. "Ben, bring me some ax handles one of these days and I'll make you a trade or give you credit."

"I'll try," Ben said doubtfully, "but Pa keeps me busier'n a hen on a hot griddle."

As he turned to go, he was nearly knocked over by Will, who burst into the store excited and out of breath.

"H-have you seen Mr. Hammond?" Will stammered. "Mrs. Hawkins thought she saw him coming this way."

"What are you so stirred up about?" Ben asked.

"I ran down to his boarding place, but he's been gone for an hour," Will said anxiously. He turned back across the porch and looked up and down the street.

"Will you tell me what's the matter?" Ben demanded roughly. "I thought you were supposed to be helping Pa with the corn planting instead of running wild on the Plain."

"I'll get back as quick as I can," Will said impatiently, "but I've got to find Mr. Hammond first."

"You better let it wait," Ben warned. "I'll warrant Pa doesn't know you're down here, and with both of us gone, he'll make it hot for us when we get back. I don't relish the thought of extra work just because you can't tend to business. Now go on back up the hill. You can see your precious schoolmaster after chores tonight!"

"*You* hurry back!" Will said hotly. "I'm going to find Mr. Hammond."

Ben's temper flared. He didn't want to go back just yet. He'd been of a mind to go home by way of Arnold's Falls, and that would take time. He fastened a hand on Will's shoulder and shook him.

"Now, I've had enough of your mysterious poppycock. What's the reason you can't wait till later?"

Will twisted angrily. "That's my business! I don't have to do your bidding! Let me alone!"

"Ben Tanner, leave your bother be!" commanded a waspish voice behind Ben.

He scowled over his shoulder at Letty Barber, who frowned right back.

"I can take care of this," he said shortly.

"That's broad as 'tis long," she retorted. "Now take your hands off Will!"

"*You* don't have to stick your long nose into it!" Ben shouted.

"Well, *somebody* needs to teach you some manners!" Letty squawked.

Will still squirmed at the end of Ben's arm, but he finally managed to get loose. His face was scarlet, and his shirt tail was pulled halfway out. Ben made a lunge for him, but Will dodged, and Ben found himself facing the indignant look of the schoolmaster. Angrily he tried to push Mr. Hammond aside, but the schoolmaster's hands grabbed, his broad shoulders heaved, and Ben landed on his back in the wet ruts with a thump that took his breath away.

Furiously he scrambled to his feet and tore into his black-coated antagonist. This time he sailed half across the road and lit on his shoulder. Dirty water splashed his face. He sat up coughing and rubbing at his eye.

"Why don't you sit there a minute," suggested Mr. Hammond, pulling down his cuffs. "Here's a handkerchief. Now let's have an end to brawling and see if we can straighten out this contretemps."

Unbelievingly, Ben stared upward at the unmussed schoolmaster. His dazed glance traveled to Will and Letty, who were still standing to one side. He mopped his face with the handkerchief, then got to his feet.

"As I came up, I believe I heard some discourteous remarks addressed to this lady," Mr. Hammond said sternly. "I think the first move should be an apology."

Ben stared uncertainly at Letty. He licked his lips and swallowed twice. He glanced again at the uncompromising face of the schoolmaster and finally said in a subdued voice, "Beg pardon, Lettice."

Lettice suddenly turned red. Twisting her hands in her apron, she said, "Pshaw, Ben, I should have kept to myself anyway." She turned and bolted for the store.

"Common courtesy is everyone's due," the schoolmaster stated flatly. "Rudeness is not a sign of toughness but of ignorance."

Ben rubbed his neck and was silent.

"Mr. Hammond?" Will said uncertainly.

"Yes, Will," the schoolmaster answered, turning his attention to the pale-faced boy.

"Mr. Hammond, I was trying to find you," Will said with suppressed excitement. He drew a piece of paper from his pocket and held it out. "I found this in the book you brought me last night. I knew you'd miss it, so I hurried to bring it to you."

Mr. Hammond took the paper, gave it a quick glance, and smiled. "Thanks, my boy, for your concern, but this piece of paper is valuable only as a bookmark, which was how I was using it."

"But, sir, it's a five-dollar note! I thought you'd hidden it in the book for safekeeping."

Mr. Hammond laughed. "It's true I wouldn't want it to

fall into other hands. Unhappily, though, this currency has little value. It's a forgery."

Ben stepped closer to look at the bill, his anger forgotten. Neither he nor Will had ever seen money in such a large denomination before. Even the shillings and pence and occasional Spanish coins in common use were seldom seen in town. Business transactions were almost always simple exchanges of trade goods.

Curiously the two boys examined the note. *Five (5) dol.* was written large across each end. In the middle was a picture, rather mixed up Ben thought, of some people camping beside a stream. An almost leafless tree flung its limbs over them. An eagle and shield trimmed the bottom of the paper, and there were flourishing and unreadable signatures by the cashier and president of the bank that issued the note.

Ben was torn between awe and ridicule. It was a clumsy-looking piece of work, but a genuine note of this amount was more money than he had ever owned.

"It's really not a bad imitation," Mr. Hammond was saying. "As you see, it entitles the bearer to receive five dollars in gold or silver." With his finger he traced the design. "See there, and that line in the corner? Those marks are not on the genuine five-dollar note. Apparently the engraver had trouble making that spiral, and in the corner his engraving tool slipped just a little."

"I've heard that counterfeiters are hanged!" Will exclaimed.

"Sometimes. The government is doing its best to build up confidence in the new currency, but the fact that there are so many imitations in circulation makes many people hesitate to accept paper money. We have three sound banks now, the Bank of North America, the Bank of New York, and the Massachusetts Bank. This note is supposed to be one of those issued by the Bank of North America. Genuine notes from any of these banks are backed by good reserves. If we could be sure that all the available paper money was authentic, think how much more convenient it would be for tradesmen. The country's growing economy will depend more and more on trade, and that in turn will flourish only if the problems of distribution and currency are surmounted."

"Luther Chickering wears a belt that he keeps money in when he travels," Ben volunteered. "He says it gets mighty cumbersome. Paper money wouldn't be such a drag on him."

"That's true, though people rarely find their riches a burden," Mrs. Hammond observed. "Well, I must be on my way. Thank you for your trouble, Will. Benjamin, I trust you'll not be lamed by your—ah—fall."

Ben brushed at the dirt on his rough towcloth shirt and studied his feet. Suddenly he looked up. "I just crave to know, sir," he burst out, "how did you *do* it?"

Mr. Hammond chuckled and clapped him on the shoulder. "My boy, higher education is a wonderful thing," he said. "At Dartmouth I learned Latin, Greek, calculus, and *wrestling.*" He strode away, whistling.

Ben looked sharply at Will, but the younger boy's expression was blank. "You better not think anything's cause for laughing," he warned.

Will's face looked even more blank. "No, Ben."

"I doubt that wrestling lessons would do anything for you."

"No, Ben."

Ben picked up his package and they turned toward home. Will kept straggling behind, but Ben couldn't be sure whether it was because he was so puny or because he was having trouble keeping his face straight.

VI

Ben's Big Chance

Ben left the row of onions he was planting and went to the water bucket. Inside the cabin he could hear Mrs. Johnson talking sixteen to the dozen.

"—With a splint on his leg, and still two days from home," she was saying.

"What a pity," Ma said. "It must have been hard on Luther."

Ben skidded in through the open door. "Did you say Luther, Ma? Did Luther Chickering break his leg?"

"My stars!" Mrs. Johnson clucked disapprovingly. "You certainly give a body a turn, bursting in that way."

Ben shook his head impatiently. "I thought I heard . . ."

His mother interrupted him. "Benjamin, since you're here, will you put a stick on the fire?" She had taken her pewter teapot from the corner cupboard and was dropping pinches of tea into it with great care.

Ben slammed a piece of birch wood into the fireplace and turned again to his mother, but Mrs. Johnson was still talking. "I just can't understand why anyone would leave his own bed and wander off to wicked places like Montreal and Boston—sleeping on the ground, menaced by varmints and robbers, exposed to fevers—oh, my!" She stopped for breath, apparently overcome by her own imagination.

"Ma?" Ben begged, desperation in his voice.

"No, son, it wasn't Luther," his mother said. "It was Plin."

"Plin broke his leg!" A wonderful idea blossomed in Ben's mind. His face stretched in a delighted grin, then sobered quickly as he caught Mrs. Johnson's reproving look. He stepped over to the hearth and poked with the tongs at the fresh stick he had placed there.

If Plin had a broken leg, he couldn't travel with Luther for a long time. The trader would have to get someone else to help him, especially with the huge load he'd be carrying on the next trip. Ben's heart thudded. He'd have to find Luther right away, before he took on someone else.

Ben whirled around and interrupted the indignant Mrs. Johnson once again.

"Where is Luther now?" he inquired eagerly. "Where did they take Plin?"

"Last I knew, they were at Arnold's Mills," Mrs. Johnson said tartly. "That's where my Lem saw them. Luther was unloading some things."

Ben had stopped listening. "Ma, I have to go on down to the Mills and see if I can catch Luther. I'll finish the garden after supper."

"Get along, you great gawk," said his mother in an exasperated tone. "I'm bound we can do without you!"

Ben leaped through the door and set off at a lope, his moccasins leaving deep prints in the soft dirt of the path. His thoughts flew even faster than his feet. If only Luther would take him on for one trip—just one! A trip would show the trader how far superior he was as a trail companion compared to the scrawny, whining boy now nursing a broken leg. Probably Plin had done something stupid like falling out of the wagon. Plin couldn't even yoke up an ox without spraining his wrist.

Flushed and panting, Ben thudded to a stop in front of the sawmill. Luther's wagon stood before the open structure, his team patiently switching flies. The wagon was partially unloaded, Ben noted, so Luther must have brought some goods for the sawyer. There was no sign of Plin.

Luther slouched tiredly as he stood talking to David Bowen and Horace Cutler. Ben gave a smothered yelp of dismay. How could he talk to Luther with Mr. Cutler listening in? As he hesitated, Luther left the two men and walked to the side of the wagon. He shoved a couple of barrels away from the tailgate. Ben was quick to give him a hand. Luther eyed him curiously and bobbed his shaggy head.

"Much obliged," he said in his high, thin voice.

Ben dusted his hands and was suddenly speechless. So much depended on his question that he couldn't get it out.

Luther's broad chest swelled with a sigh of weariness. His greasy leather vest and frayed homespun breeches were streaked with mud, and lines of fatigue were knit around his eyes. Luther's pale gray eyes, like his high voice, were surprising in such a rough-looking man. Now they were red-rimmed and dull, and as Ben looked at them his heart sank. He never should have come when Luther was tired and in poor spirits. He would be in no mood to have Ben pestering him again. Still, now that he was here, he had to say something or be thought a ninny.

"I heard about Plin," he said uncertainly.

"It was a bad business," Luther said grimly. "He had a rough ride, and it was mortal hard on the oxen, too. They've traveled without rest for nineteen hours."

Ben wondered why Luther didn't count himself in on the hard journey. He had walked those nineteen hours, too, keeping the tired team moving along the rocky track. Anyone less familiar with the route would have had to stop for the night.

Ben took a deep breath. "Mr. Chickering, you'll need someone else to help out when you—that is, till Plin gets better," he said. "Pa doesn't need me much now—he's been sending me to school, even." Ben gulped. "I'm *much* stronger than Plin," he added earnestly.

Luther rubbed his whiskers with a mud-caked hand. *"Mister* Chickering, is it?" he asked. "Nobody never calls me that without they want something. So you're not busy enough, eh?"

"No, sir. I mean, yes, sir. I'm busy—I'm not lazy. But I could get away."

"Well, lad, it's true I'm in a spot," Luther mused. "Do you think you can obey orders?"

"Yes, sir!" Ben yelled. He barely kept himself from dancing. Traders' assistants didn't frolic in the mud.

Heavy steps came toward them, and Horace Cutler clapped Luther on the shoulder. In his broadcloth coat and shining boots, he was a sharp contrast to the bedraggled traveler.

"You'll be going out again soon?" Cutler asked. "I have a good hundred-weight of potash processed and ready for you."

"Aye," Luther said wearily. "Give me a few days to rest the cattle and see how Betsy and the boys have fared with the planting. Ben here will take Plin's place."

Cutler's face twisted slightly as though he had bitten down on something sour. "Now, Luther," he said, "have you thought enough on such a course? We all know Ben to be an able lad, but rather given to—ah—impatience."

"Ben's some excitable, maybe," Luther agreed, "but I've been keeping bull calves in line for years, and I reckon I can keep him pointed in the right direction."

"I don't want to meddle in your business," Cutler said, his tone acquiring a faintly fretful edge, "but those goods you carry belong to me and to others of the town. That makes your business our business, too. I deem it a rash act to take on a bumptious boy who shows little self-control and a proved lack of respect for authority." Cutler threw Ben a black glance.

A lump of ice formed in Ben's stomach, as Luther gave him a thoughtful look. Was he going to change his mind because of that fat meddler? If Cutler spoiled his chance to go with Luther, Ben vowed he would flatten him.

"I'll be in charge of the goods—not Ben," Luther said mildly.

"You don't know the risk you're taking," Cutler insisted roughly. "I've traveled a good amount and I know the dangers in letting a hot-tempered, unlettered bumpkin run wild in a town full of shysters and footpads."

Luther's pale eyes flashed. "I'm too spent to bandy words," he said, his high voice squeaking with irritation. "If you can't help dwelling on the dangers of Portland Town and Boston, perhaps you'd better leave your potash off my load. Ben will go with me. I need someone with a strong back for these boneshaking roads, and if his mind is weak, no matter. Ben's willing, and I'd take him even if he had two heads!"

Luther stamped around to the side of the off ox and left Ben gnawing his lip, uncertain whether to be pleased or angry. Cutler stalked back to the mill without looking behind him.

Then Luther goaded his patient team into the road. Heads dipping, they planted careful feet in the slippery hillside and started the heavy wagon creaking toward the crest. Ben followed along.

Halfway up, Luther paused. "Whoa, Buck. Easy, Star. No hurry, boys." The oxen stopped in mid-stride and stood, their wet red and white sides heaving.

"Will your Pa really be of a mind to do without you?" Luther asked as he mopped his face.

"Spring's work is about finished," Ben answered. "I'm certain he'll not object!" Privately, Ben wished that he could be sure. How could he bear it if Pa, having considered the move in his methodical way, said no. There would be no ifs, ands, or buts once his father's decision was made.

"Hish, Star!" Luther called, and touched the flanks of the oxen with his goad. The wagon rumbled forward, its axles squealing. Luther wouldn't have taken time to grease them, Ben thought.

At the end of their slow journey, Luther guided his load to the rear of Amaziah Barber's store. Lettice came to the back door. "Here's ham and bread, Luther. Come in and sit down," she ordered sharply.

Luther settled his black wreck of a hat and shook his head. "I'd be obliged if you'd just let me lug the vittles with me," he said in his scratchy trebel. "I'll poke along home and get out of these boots. I vow, Betsy will have a time getting me into 'em again."

"If that's what you want, go to it," Lettice said tartly. Her apron crackled as she got the food from the table and handed it out through the door. "Plin's sleeping," she said. "I scraped some dandelion roots and brewed him a draught."

"Plin's here?" Ben asked with surprise.

"And why not?" Lettice snapped.

"Why, that's fine," Ben said hastily. "Jingo, that's—that's fine!" He didn't intend to stub his toe on *her* again.

"I'll be back for the wagon come noon tomorrow," Luther said as he turned away.

"Pa will have it unloaded, and he'll take care of the team," Lettice promised.

Ben stepped silently beside Luther along the sun-dappled road that wound upward from the Plain. Three miles or so northward, Luther's narrow house sat snugly on a slope above the rushing Sleeper's River.

Now, as they came to the path that led to Ben's own dooryard, both stopped. "Give me word tomorrow, boy," Luther wheezed.

"I will. Don't you worry," Ben said positively. Watching Luther's figure move on up the road, he realized ruefully that it wasn't Luther who was worrying.

He hurried back to the unfinished garden row on which he had been working. Hoeing vigorously, he loosened and smoothed the dark plowed ground. Right there where he had had so much trouble uprooting a reluctant old beech stump would be a good place for the pumpkin bed, he decided.

Finally he went to the cabin. "You can sprout your pumpkin seed now, Ma," he informed his mother. "The bed's all ready." Ma liked to wrap the pumpkin seeds in a wet towel and set them aside until sprouts had formed before planting them.

His mother turned from the fireplace where she was stirring a kettle and wiped her red eyes on the hem of her apron. "Ben, something's got to be done about that chimney!" she fretted. "I declare, the smoke gets worse every day."

"Pa said come fall, we'd build a brick chimney," Ben reminded her absently, his mind on his own problems. "Be sure you put the seeds where they'll sprout real fast."

"Well, I can't hurry them too much—I don't want to *cook* them," his mother said with an exasperated edge to her voice. "Goodness knows, the rain has held back planting enough this spring, but what's the sudden rush to get the pumpkins planted?"

Ben eyed her apprehensively. He hadn't counted on her being upset. Right now, he wanted someone on *his* side. Suddenly his mother burst into laughter.

"Oh, Ben, you big goose! Stop looking so downcast. You look exactly as you used to when you thought someone was going to take away your toys."

Ben managed a grin. "Well, you know Luther . . ." he said awkwardly.

"That's a statement I can't deny," she said dryly. "Now let me guess the rest. Since Plin can't travel, Luther has decided at long last that you will be the perfect trail companion. You'll be leaving for faraway places in a day or two."

"I guess it's not all quite like that," Ben said, remembering Luther's remark about two heads. Then his enthusiasm broke out again. "Ma, he *did* say I could go. This time I can go!"

"If your father agrees."

"You think he will, don't you? We won't have to leave for about a week. I can finish the garden and do anything else you want done. Maybe I can clean out the chimney."

"When I was about your age, I wanted to go to Philadelphia," his mother said with a faraway look in her eyes. "I hoped I might visit Cousin Belle and perhaps get to see the fine gentlemen and ladies going to a ball. Belle wrote about their beautiful silk dresses and their jewels. Through the windows of the big houses, she could sometimes see the candles shining—hundreds of them—and she could hear the music."

"I guess Portland has fine houses, too," Ben ventured.

"Oh, I'm sure it does. There are beautiful tall houses with carving on the gables. Inside are marvelous things that sailing men have brought back from all over the world—ivory and glass and teakwood."

"I'd surely like to see them," Ben said eagerly.

His mother straightened her apron with a determined jerk. "You let me speak to your father, Benjamin," she said firmly. "Just you go after the cows now and don't worry."

So, to Ben's thrilled delight, consent was granted for his journey without a word of pleading on his part. Will was overcome with admiration. Goody was also overcome, but with fears for the dangers Ben would certainly face. His mother worried aloud as she assembled and reassembled his clothing. His father offered advice and guidance. Through it all, Ben moved in a golden haze, his head filled with anticipation of the days ahead.

VII

A Bad Beginning

※◈◎◈※

When Luther's wagon finally hove into sight at the end of the Plain, Ben was nearly in a state of collapse. He had been waiting for hours, although his father had pointed out before Ben left home that Luther couldn't possibly reach St. Johnsbury before nine o'clock. Luther had planned to swing around through Danville Green the day before to pick up a few trade items, and then to meet Ben at Barber's Store.

It seemed to Ben that he had been sitting on the edge of the Barbers' narrow porch, watching and worrying, long enough for Luther to go halfway to Portland. He leaned his head on his calloused palms and groaned.

A light patter of rain hit the ground and caused him to raise his eyes to the gray sky. It was then that he saw the team plodding toward him with Luther striding loose-kneed beside them. Behind the wagon ambled a sway-backed horse and a cow. Both of them carried packs. Ben was still staring when Luther waved his goad and stopped the team.

"Here I am," Luther announced, "and here you are, so let's get Amaziah's goods aboard."

"What—what's that you've got tied on behind the wagon?"

Ben demanded, staring at the sad-eyed cow. "I thought you didn't drive cattle till fall."

Luther said cheerfully, "That's so. But Frank Shaw was powerful anxious for me to take his potash to market and knew I didn't have room, so he figured out his own transportation. Don't doubt that when we get to the wharves, some ship will take the 'transportation' aboard for the food lockers."

Together Ben and Luther filled every corner and cranny of the wagon with barrels, tubs, and bundles from Amaziah's back room. When the load was lashed snugly, Luther tramped into the small bedroom where Plin lay on the bed, one leg a stiff ridge under the quilt. His thin, lopsided face had a bluish tinge against the pillows. His black hair hung uncombed and lank over his ears.

"Now don't go running off," Luther told him.

Plin didn't seem to find humor in the remark. Ben peered over Luther's shoulder and wished he could think of something to say. He felt an unexpected warmth for the scrawny boy, for he was obviously in pain.

"Letty will take good care of you," Ben said.

Plin turned cloudy black eyes his way. "You watch your step," he sneered, "or those Portland boys will have your britches."

Ben stiffened. "Don't you worry about me," he muttered. In his pack were a few items he meant to trade on his own, and privately he felt that he would make a good thing of it.

Luther said an abrupt good-by and took up his goad. "Better trail behind for a spell," he advised Ben, "and see that the pack animals behave."

With no further ceremony, they were on the trail. Ben was vaguely disappointed. It seemed as though there should have been some sort of a send-off—maybe a cheer or two. He felt keenly that the little caravan lacked distinction.

They made their slow way down Sand Hill, crossed the

Passumpsic at Arnold's Mills, and set out along the steep, winding road toward East Village. Nobody noticed their passing in the drizzling rain.

"Seems as if whoever laid out this road looked for the highest hills he could find and ran the tracks slap over the top," grumbled Luther as he dropped back to brake the wheels of the heavily loaded wagon.

Their splayed feet slipping on the muddy stones, the oxen drew the rumbling wagon down another steep pitch. A complaining moo came from the following cow.

"Lay hold of her tail, Ben," Luther shouted back. "Likely she wants braking, too!"

Ben knocked the water out of his hat brim and said nothing.

After about three miles, they turned south toward Waterford and the Connecticut River. The weather cleared after an hour or so, but when they stood on the bank of the tumbling barrier between Vermont and New Hampshire, it didn't look at all inviting. Ben frowned as he watched the muddied waters sweeping by.

Luther stuck his thumbs under his armpits and teetered on his heels as he surveyed the scene. "Well, it'll likely be worse before it's better," he commented stoically. "Let's eat, anyhow."

They drew a little away from the short rough street that lay along a natural shelf paralleling the river. Luther dropped the yoke and untied the pack animals. Cold sausage and cornbread out of the provision box tasted wonderful to famished Ben. He was licking up the last crumb when he remembered a rhubarb tart that his mother had tucked into his bag. He divided the pastry with Luther, then set out to explore the river bank while Luther smoked his pipe.

The rush of the gray water worried him. Since the little town had grown up, the ford had been constantly in use, but all the same, he didn't like the looks of it.

"Hitch 'em up!" Luther called.

Ben walked to the roadside where the steers were snatching mouthfuls of grass. He put his arm over Buck's neck and guided him back to the wagon. He shoved the bow under the steer's chin, leaned the yoke over it, and slammed in the bowpin.

"Star, come here now," he said firmly, but Star didn't feel like leaving the green grass. Taking the goad, Ben walked over and rapped him on the shoulder. With great deliberation, the massive ox stepped over and ranged up beside Buck. Ben attached the chain between them.

Then he went to fetch the horse and, finally, the cow. "Come on, Clara," he told the gaunt creature, "we're going for a little walk." She stared at him and lowed mournfully.

Snorting and rolling their eyes, the oxen started their careful way down the gravel bank and into the river. As the wheels surged under the water, the pack horse reared and tried to hang back. The wagon bumped over the rocky bottom. Luther waded ahead, a frown of concentration on his dark face as he probed the depths with his goad.

The gray, racing current boiled against the stout wagon body and pushed against Ben's legs. His moccasins were infernally slippery. Then the horse reared again, whinnying with fright. Ben splashed forward and grabbed the halter, pulling the animal down, but he lunged again, lifting Ben half out of the water and slamming him hard against the wagon.

As the breath was knocked out of him, Ben's fingers slipped from the halter and he disappeared under the water. He felt his body turning over and over as the current swept him along. His knee smashed into a rock, and a searing pain shot along his leg. Frantically he thrust out his arms, trying to get a grip on something. Then the roar of water in his ears faded away and there was only blackness.

A great cough wrenched Ben's chest, and his eyes flew open

to stare at wavelets only inches from his nose. He coughed and gagged again, and he felt something hard digging into his stomach. Then, as his senses steadied, he realized that he was slung over Luther's shoulder. His head was hanging alongside the bulky man's belt and only just clearing the water as Luther packed him across the river. Twisting his neck, he caught a glimpse of Buck and Star faithfully following.

"Quit squirming, else I'll dump you in the drink again," Luther wheezed.

"Put me down," Ben demanded weakly.

"Nothing doing," Luther said grimly. "I don't plan to fish you out twice." He sloshed steadily along with Ben flopping miserably against his back, and finally Ben was dumped roughly onto the muddy bank.

"Welcome to New Hampshire," Luther said and turned back to his team without a second look. He urged the streaming oxen up the bank to a level spot and spoke roughly to the skittish horse. Then he checked the cow, still placid but as melancholy as ever.

Meanwhile, Ben slumped dejectedly on the bank, trying to catch his breath. He slipped off his hunting coat and tried to wring some of the water out of the sleeves. Gingerly he touched the swelling on his knee. What a wonder on the trail he'd turned out to be! Hardly out of town and he'd already banged himself up and maybe endangered the load. Luther must be real pleased with his choice of a helper. Ben scrambled painfully to his feet as Luther approached.

Luther planted his feet wide and surveyed his shivering assistant. "You look worse than the cow," he said. "Can you travel?"

Ben limped around in a small circle. His side hurt where he'd hit the wagon box and his knee was getting stiff. Walking would probably help limber it up, he thought.

"I'm all right," he muttered. He held up his coat, wondering whether the wet thing would have any warmth in it. His leather breeches were cold and slimy, and he knew that when they dried, they'd be so stiff they wouldn't bend without crackling. Also, his hat was gone.

In a burst of anger and disappointment, he flung the coat on the ground. "That blasted horse has got to learn some manners," he shouted hoarsely.

Luther nodded. "Maybe it was *his* first crack at the Connecticut, too. Now you both step out proper, and we won't have trouble."

Ben got his first look at New Hampshire as he tramped along in his squishing moccasins. With a blanket bundled around his shoulders, he plodded listlessly through chuckholes in the road, following Luther's squat figure and the rocking wagon. On the rare occasions when he lifted his eyes from the twisting path, he was unimpressed with the view. Looked just like a slice of Vermont—more steep hillsides, more granite boulders, more tall trees.

The gray afternoon wore into gray evening, and they saw fellow travelers only twice. Once a lean, pock-marked man carrying a sack of grain on his shoulder caught up to them and passed on with a brief nod. Later they met an ox cart. On the plank seat rode a small, withered grandmother in a sunbonnet, and Luther touched his hat.

"Yonder is Moses Little's settlement," Luther called, pointing ahead with the goad.

Ben just grunted without enthusiasm.

Luther dropped back. He wiped his lined face on his sleeve. "Reckon we'll put up at the inn, where the cattle will have a dry place to rest. It's been a slow day, but they've done sixteen miles and it's been tarnation slippery all the way."

Ben thought stopping under a roof sounded like a fine idea. His knee was paining him and he was footsore and weary. The edge of the rough blanket had worn a sore spot on the back of his neck, and the wet buckskins had chafed his legs. He took off the blanket, folded it, and put it on top of the wagon. His blue shirt was nearly dry from the heat of his body.

"Gee, Star! Come around," Luther directed, and the wagon rumbled into the stable yard behind the inn. Ben forgot his own discomfort as he hurried back and forth from the watering trough to the haymow, caring for the needs of the patient animals. Even the horse was too tired to give him any trouble.

Luther was hailed from the back steps with the familiarity that told of long acquaintance. "Glad to see you back," exclaimed the man whom Ben took to be the innkeeper. He turned and bawled through the open door, "Fanny, set a place for Chickering and his boy! Make sure the pot's hot!"

"Evening, Alphy," Luther said agreeably. He laid his hat on the wide bench that was placed beside the door, tipped water into a basin, and washed up with snorting satisfaction.

After Ben had done the same, he followed Luther into the big room. It was gay with red and yellow light from the huge fireplace and heavy with the smell of wet woolens, candle tallow, and roasting pork. Across the end of the room, a long table was set with wooden plates and mugs. Luther and Ben straddled the bench and sat down facing two men who were already busy at their meal.

One of them had on as slick a suit of clothes as Ben had ever seen. He had a short, neat beard, clipped in a style that Ben had never seen before, and a ring that flashed when he lifted his knife. The other man was apparently an elderly farmer. He had a pink scar over one eye that made his eyelid droop.

In the corner, an enormously plump woman stirred a kettle and talked to herself in little spurts of sound. She bustled over to the table and put down generous servings of Indian pudding and boiled greens. Still muttering to herself, she hurried away and returned with a platter of smoked salmon.

"Ah, look at that salmon!" chortled Luther, wiping his mouth with the back of his hand.

"It's good," mumbled Ben.

"Catch them around here?" asked the well-dressed traveler, daintily sampling the pink fish.

"Not so far from here—on the Ammonoosuc River," Luther explained. "There's an outcropping ledge on the south bank where the river has undercut and made a deep hole. Salmon weighing twenty-five pounds come out of there. It used to be a favorite fishing place for the Indians—they salted 'em down for the winter."

"You seem to be well acquainted with this area," remarked the traveler. "Do you know St. Johnsbury?"

"I'm a mite knowledgeable about the towns around here," admitted Luther.

"I'll be in St. Johnsbury tomorrow," said the stranger. "Oh—Grimes is my name, tailoring my trade."

Luther introduced himself and Ben. Ben jerked his head in a self-conscious nod.

"I have a little business in Caledonia County," Grimes continued, smiling expansively. "Fine men in your neck of the woods. Don't take the narrow point of view. Going places."

Luther went on eating. After a bit, Ben sneaked a look at Mr. Grimes, who was relaxing after his meal. He unbuttoned his bright waistcoat, which had been pulled tight over a little round stomach. Ben wondered what such a fine-looking gentleman wanted in these parts.

Over in the chimney corner, Fanny, the plump cook, was talking to herself again. Ben strained to understand the petulant sputtering, so he didn't notice when Luther stood up.

"You going to eat all night, Ben?" Luther asked with a grin.

Ben jumped up so quickly that he banged against the table and made the plates clatter. He followed Luther into the small adjoining room where the other men were lounging in front of the fireplace and talking with their host.

VIII

A Mysterious Visitor

Along one wall, a steep, narrow staircase led to the upstairs rooms. Luther dropped into a splint-bottomed chair near the foot of the stairs and tilted it comfortably against the wall. Ben didn't want to elbow into the ring around the fire, so he took a seat on the bottom step.

Tacked to the opposite wall was a badly lettered sign proclaiming the rules of the house:

No shoes to be worn in bed
No dogs allowed upstairs
Breakfast before 5:00 or go empty

"Couldn't stop old Matt Lyon," said the farmer with the scarred face. "In he jumped and off he went! Just left the sheriff standing there staring after the sleigh."

"But why didn't the sheriff take after Lyon and arrest him?" queried Alphy. "He had the new warrant right in his pocket."

"He couldn't! Congress was in session already, and Lyon had been reelected Congressman from Western Vermont while he was in jail. Immunity, they call it. Congressional immunity."

"That was last February," Alphy mused. "What's old Matt doing now?"

"He's down in Philadelphia keeping things hot in the House of Representatives for President Adams' pompous pets."

"Have you seen anything that he's written lately?"

"No, but I bet he's still at it. Did you see the one in the *Gazette* where he called the Federalists contemptible, cowardly, and treacherous? There was some more to it, but I forget the words."

Ben searched his mind for facts about Congressman Lyon and wished that he had paid more attention when his father and the neighbors were discussing the rebellious Irishman. He did know that Lyon believed strongly—and loudly—in Vice-President Thomas Jefferson's new party. He raged at the Federalist belief that only the well-born and well-educated were capable of governing wisely. Jefferson's faith that the common man had sense enough to have a voice in his government was spreading fast—to the great alarm of the Federalists—and Lyon was always in the forefront of the attack on the well-to-do merchants, bankers, and landowners who had entrenched themselves in the government.

"Mark my words," the elegant Grimes said severely, "no good will come of such malicious charges as Lyon is expounding. Irresponsible reporting of the facts will tend to lower respect for our governing bodies and lead to bloody anarchy such as the French are experiencing."

The old farmer bristled. "You call it anarchy if the farmers and tradesmen cry out against heavy taxes? Taxes levied to pay for more waste and extravagance by John Adams' swaggering nincompoops!" The old man's mustaches twitched violently.

"You yourself have all the marks of Matthew Lyon's seditious associates, my good sir," Grimes said coldly. "Your unconsidered words only prove my point. We need a strong national government—a bulwark against the ignorant lackeys who forever shout about extravagance simply because they do not have the wit to get their own hands in the coffer."

The farmer jumped to his feet and thrust out his stiff old hands. "My hands are cleaner than the grasping claws in the capital!" he stormed. "How clean are the hands of those who are beating the drum for war with France? Those who link Jefferson with the French Revolutionists just because he's sympathetic with the French people and their struggle to rid themselves of the aristocrats!"

"Here, now," Luther said mildly, "this is no debating hall."

The old man subsided into his chair, then jerked it halfway around so that his back was toward the others. Grimes sat stiffly, fingering his smooth chin and staring sternly into the fire. He certainly looked angry.

Ben began to wonder about the older man. For a farmer, he seemed to get around a lot. He apparently knew a good deal about what went on in politics, and he could talk about it, too.

Soon Luther heaved himself out of his chair and yawned. "Let's check the beasts," he said. "I'm ready for Alphy's corncob and sawdust mattress." He winked at Ben.

Alphy looked pained. "Why, my mattresses are filled with the best straw off the threshing floor every fall," he protested. "You'll sleep as sound as though you had a clear conscience."

Luther's face creased in a grin, and he tramped off to the shed. Buck and Star were lying down, their heavy sides swelling with their even breathing. Buck turned his head briefly, and the light gleamed on the sweep of his horns. After a quick look at the wagon, Luther and Ben went back to the kitchen.

Luther lifted down the notched wooden bootjack from its peg on the wall and tucked one heel firmly between the prongs. Then, standing on the end of the board with his other foot, he pulled his foot slowly out of his boot. "Ah," he breathed, wiggling his toes. He repeated the job with the other boot, and slid the jack along to Ben.

"For these?" Ben asked in surprise. His moccasins were almost falling off his feet.

Fanny came bustling over and took Luther's boots to the fire.

"Good girl, Fanny," he said. "Nobody can take care of boots the way my woman does, but you do tolerable well."

Fanny picked up Ben's moccasins and set them beside Luther's boots. "That's not good trail footgear," she mourned. She looked at his leather breeches. "Those need drying, too— my gracious me, you'll catch your death of dampness in those britches."

Ben jumped back in alarm. "They're fine, ma'am," he said hastily. "Feel fine. Good night." He made for the stairway.

The space above stairs in the inn was taken up by two small rooms, one on each side of the dark little hallway. Ben guessed that the building had been built as a dwelling, but it was now being used as a public house for the accommodation of travelers who were beginning to move through the northern woods in increasing numbers.

Shielding the candle flame with his calloused hand, Luther turned into the room on the right. Two wide bedsteads almost filled it. The ceiling slanted sharply, close overhead.

Ben took off his breeches and hung them on a bed post. He crawled under the quilt and stretched out with a sigh. As Luther draped his clothing over the other post, the old farmer came in, tested the second bed, and got into it without ceremony. His face was grim.

Luther blew out the candle, and the bed ropes creaked as he settled down beside Ben. The night was so dark that Ben couldn't even make out the tiny square of window. The old farmer was whispering to himself, and Ben didn't know whether he was calling down curses on Grimes or saying his prayers.

Well, his first day on the trail certainly hadn't turned out as he'd imagined it would, Ben thought. He wondered what Luther was thinking. It was still over a hundred miles to Portland. He had plenty of time yet to show Luther just how much help he could be on the road. As he drifted into sleep, his thoughts turned homeward, and he felt odd, lying there beside Luther in a strange, dark room. Back home, Goody would already be asleep in her low bed. Likely, Pa would have banked the fire and sent Will up the ladder. Ma would have set the dough for tomorrow's bread to rise on the shelf under the window. Ben turned impatiently and drew the quilt around his ears. He certainly was glad he wasn't one of those dull, stay-at-home folks, he told himself firmly.

The pink sky of early dawn filled the little window when Ben woke. The farmer in the bed across the room still slept, snoring gently, but Luther was already struggling into his clothes. Ben sprang out of bed, shivering as his feet touched the cold floor, and reached for his own breeches. The bed post was empty. He squinted to see where they might have fallen but couldn't spy them. He knelt and looked under the bed. Still no breeches. Heavy-eyed and surly, Luther opened the door and headed downstairs in his stocking feet. Ben threw back the quilt and examined the folds. Nothing. He could hear the rattle of the kettle chain from below and could smell wood smoke. Then he heard slow steps on the stairs. Fanny!

Wild-eyed, Ben looked for a place to hide. The room didn't have a cupboard or a chest in it. He jumped back into bed and pulled the covers clear over his head. The wide floorboards creaked as Fanny came into the room.

"So here they are, nice and dry. My stars and garters, where's he got to?"

In the bed, Ben quivered under his covering. Heavy breathing filled the silence for a minute. Then, still muttering gently, Fanny turned and shuffled back to the door.

As he heard her go down the steep staircase, Ben also heard the door of the other bedchamber open. A different set of footsteps echoed in the hall, paused at Ben's door, and then continued toward him. It was Ben's turn to be perplexed. Was it Grimes? He knew of no other guest in the upstairs room. If it was Grimes, what was he doing in here?

Sunk in the loose mattress, his lean length covered with the tumbled quilt, Ben strained his ears and wished he dared peek out. He was sure the steps had stopped at the opposite bed.

"Still sleeping—the seditious old fool," came a grim whisper. It *was* the polished traveling man. Ben guessed the angry old man in the next bed must be a little deaf. None of the comings and goings had wakened him.

The whisper came again. "I'll leave him a gift he isn't expecting." Ben heard a tiny crackle of paper. He lay rigid, wondering if Grimes was going to harm the old fellow. Cautiously he eased the quilt away from his face. It was Grimes, all right, but Ben saw only his back as the man crossed the room and thudded down the stairs.

As soon as he was securely clad in his breeches, Ben scuttled through the kitchen and joined Luther in the back yard. The morning was fresh and clear. Luther leaned against the wagon, scratching his head and contemplating the barn swallows that were venturing out to greet the day.

Eastward, twenty-five miles away, the peaks of the White Hills stood dark and blue in the clear air. The tallest of them was capped in shimmering white. A red rooster stepped importantly out of the shed, threw back his head, and crowed.

"He doesn't seem to realize he overslept," Luther said dryly. "You two make a good pair."

"I was awake!" Ben protested. "I had trouble finding my

clothes," he added hastily. *That* made him sound like a down-right idiot. His face grew red. "Well, Fanny . . ." He stopped in confusion.

Luther eyed him blackly.

"The first thing I do after we get to Portland is get me some more britches!" Ben yelled.

Luther's laughter followed him as he stomped across to the back steps.

Ben would have preferred not to face any of the people in the house, but his stomach wouldn't let him stay away from the breakfast table. Actually it was a quick and quiet meal. Everyone was preoccupied and anxious to get on the road. The innkeeper drank from a steaming cup that he carried about, not bothering to sit down. The old farmer didn't appear at all.

Luther took an order from Alphy for merchandise to be brought back from Portland. Alphy warned Ben not to let the city girls catch him and laughed.

Then they were on the road again, the sun in their eyes as they swung out of Littleton toward the White Hills. Just outside of town they reached the banks of the Ammonoosuc. It was a much smaller stream than the Connecticut and, to Ben's tremendous relief, the crossing gave them no trouble.

Not far beyond the river, the road forked and one branch turned due south. Luther stopped the rocking wagon and jerked his head toward the southern tracks.

"Franconia that way," he volunteered. "Awful rough going. Lots of landslides. Got a mountain down there that beats all. It's got a rock face that *is* a face. Got a mighty square jaw, but it's a man's face right enough."

"Why don't we go that way?" Ben asked.

Luther shook his head. "The other way—by way of the notch—is much better for getting to Portland."

The wagon rattled forward again. A few miles of easy trav-eling brought them to Bethlehem, its name proclaimed by a wooden marker at the side of the road. Luther tramped past the little cluster of buildings, responding to a couple of hails with a wave of his goad. Apparently he had no business here—at least not on this trip.

At noon they stopped at a natural clearing in the woods. Here they turned the animals out to graze, ate the bread and salt pork that Fanny had provided, and lay back among white, furry stems of Indian tobacco for a brief rest.

Ben wasn't sleepy. His eyes followed the clouds, scudding high and white above the tossing crest of a towering elm. That same west wind was going on, over the mountains, to fill the sails of a ship leaving Portland Harbor, he figured. He was impatient to reach there.

He said as much to Luther as they tramped along in the afternoon between endless lines of tree-capped ridges.

"Noisy, cluttered place," Luther commented. "Kind of interesting, but I wouldn't be able to stand the commotion for long. Don't know how the storekeepers and the men in the ropewalks and all the rest of 'em can stand it, but they do. Claim they'd go crazy back in the woods where they couldn't hear the sea or smell the salt air."

"What's a ropewalk?" Ben asked.

"Sort of a big long barn where they make rope. They store cargo there, too."

"Sure wish we could get a move on," Ben said fretfully.

"If you're in such a rush to get somewhere, you might as well take your gun and see if you can run down a rabbit," Luther remarked.

Ben was happy to drag his rifle out of the wagon and trot up the shoulder of a long ridge. He picked his way upward between gnarled old spruces, clambered along a little ledge of gray granite pitted with shining flecks of mica, and stopped under a huge beech tree.

There was rabbit sign all around. Ben stood quietly, his eyes searching the softwood thickets. Overhead the beech leaves rustled in the wind. Acting on a sudden whim, Ben leaned his gun against a rotten stump and pulled himself onto a low limb of the mountain monarch. He reached for the next hand hold and struggled upward. What a tree! It looked like fifty feet to the ground. He braced his back against the trunk and surveyed his world. Behind him wound the road, in and out of sight among the hills. Beyond that was a suggestion of the tree-lined length of the Connecticut, backed up by the hazy purple shapes of the Green Mountains. Turning again to the east, Ben's eyes took in the tumbled mass of the White Hills, much nearer now, rising ridge on rounded ridge to the bare crags of the highest one of all outlined against the milky-blue sky. How could a wagon ever get over that barrier?

His gaze traveled southward over the unbroken wilderness of trees. He saw hardwood and softwood, dark green and bright green, with cloud shadows sailing swiftly across the hills. Over there was a dark rift . . . Ben's face filled with awe. Ten miles or more away was a chasm in the hills—a vast, black ravine cutting through the blue slopes, rimmed with scars of gray rock. He stared into the distance, fascinated. It had to be the notch—the place where they were heading. With a last quick look around, he started down. Luther would begin to wonder what kind of hunter his camp tender was if he didn't hear the gun pretty soon.

When Ben trotted down out of the timber, a fat rabbit dangling from his belt, he found Luther passing the time of day with a wagoner who was headed west. The stranger's oxen were gaunt and dirty and stood with low-hanging heads.

"Whoever laid out this poor excuse for a trail ought to follow it till his dying day," the stranger was saying peevishly. He looked almost as fagged out as his beasts, Ben thought.

" 'Tis a mite rough in spots," Luther agreed. "But heard tell it's going to be improved. There's talk of forming a turnpike corporation and making it a regular highway."

The stranger spat. "Then they'll put up their pike poles, sit in their little stations, and collect money from honest working folks. Well, not from me, I'll tell you, even if I have to go by way of Jefferson Highlands!" He hit his off ox a sharp rap with the goad and creaked slowly away.

Ben fell into step beside Luther. "He seemed kind of put out," he remarked.

Luther grinned. He shoved his floppy hat back and rubbed the red welt across his forehead. "Got bested in a trade, if I don't miss my guess. Or maybe he's going home without something his wife told him to get, and he knows he's in for a tongue-lashing."

Then Luther looked serious. "Said he lost half a day chopping through a blowdown ahead of us a piece. No question about the notch trail, though—it's a poor excuse for a road."

"Say," Ben said excitedly, "I think I saw the notch."

"How could you? We've got a half-day's travel before we get there."

"I climbed a tree up on that ridge," Ben explained, pointing. "I could see a long distance."

"You don't say," Luther said thoughtfully. "Well, I've heard tell the notch was first discovered by a hunter who climbed a tree somewhere around here to look for a moose he was after. That was nigh twenty years ago."

IX

The Great Ravine

They camped late in the day near a bank of the noisy Ammonoosuc River. The trail had followed its winding valley ever since recrossing the stream at Bethlehem.

"Only one river gets in the way worse than this," grumbled Luther as he loosed the steers. "That's the Saco. We'll pick it up in the notch."

Ben grabbed the ax and hacked his way through a tangle of branches to the trunk of a fallen hardwood tree. He brought back an armful of wood and dropped it, took out his flint and steel, and swiftly set about making a fire. In no time smoke was curling, and the twigs began to crackle. He sat back on his heels and watched for a minute with a satisfied expression on his face. Then he loped down to the river bank with the water buckets. At the water's edge he stretched out on a big flat rock that still held the warmth of the sun and buried his face in the cold current. As quickly as he could, he scrambled back to the fire, thumped down the slopping pails, and pulled out his skinning knife. Swiftly he stripped the rabbit free of its pelt, and in minutes the meat was ready for the fire.

Ben glanced up as pebbles rattled under the trader's steps.

Luther sighed heavily. He leaned back on his heels and surveyed the camp. "Get the spider as soon as the fire burns down a mite," he directed.

After a little while, Ben brought the heavy black frying pan with its three small legs.

Luther browned a slice of salt pork. "Now hand me that careless young thumper," he said.

Ben watched the rabbit sizzle and felt pleased with himself. Luther wouldn't have any trouble noticing how handy his new trail companion was around camp. After they had eaten, Ben sat with his back to a tree, relaxed and contented in the growing dark. The fire had dwindled to a few coals, and Luther hunched slackly beside it, one arm thrown over a smooth rock. It seemed very quiet. The rush of the river was so much a part of the place that Ben's ears had almost forgotten it. Sometimes he could hear the soft, ripping noise made by the teeth of the animals as they grazed among the trees.

"Doesn't seem to be much traveling in these parts," he observed. "I don't believe we've seen half a dozen rigs all day."

Luther grunted. "Folks passing through the notch have to have a good reason for making the trip. Someday folks may go this way just to see the sights, but right now if you don't mind your step every minute, you end up in the bottom of a gulch."

Ben began to wonder just what was ahead of him.

Luther knocked out his pipe against a rock and got to his feet. "Nobody much uses this stretch except preachers and horse thieves and a few poor idiots like us. But just wait till we get down below. There's so much running back and forth on the roads that you'll almost have to sprout wings and fly to get to where you're going." With that, he stalked away to his bed under the wagon.

When they broke camp next morning, the dark spruces

were wrapped in blankets of mist. Ben had hard work spotting the oxen in the uncertain light, and it would be two hours before the sun topped the eastern peaks. He shivered as he rolled his bedding and settled it carefully in the wagon.

As the mist thinned, the rolling summits of the White Hills grew ever clearer and closer. The wagon jolted along the muddy track that wound through stands of maple and yellow birch. To the left, the tallest of the peaks, its bare and rocky crown towering over the others, flashed pink as the sun caught the snow field on its crown. Two lesser summits to the right of the trail brightened. Ben watched as rank upon rank of forested ridges stood out clearly on both sides of the trail. Then he looked around and found Luther's eyes on the high peak.

"Now there's a mountain for you," Luther said, noticing Ben's attention. "Granddaddy of all the White Hills."

"Has it got a name?" Ben asked.

"Not that I know of."

"Has anybody ever climbed to the top?"

"Can't say. Not an undertaking I'd want, even in the summer. A rain storm down here is just as likely to be a blizzard up there."

"Jingo!" Ben exclaimed. "I'll bet you can see a far piece—maybe even the sea."

"Well, don't let it fret you," Luther advised him. "You'll see the Atlantic in time, and a whole lot closer. Right now we have to worry about going down—not up."

The trail turned sharply southward, and Ben caught his breath as the gorge opened out before them. Great perpendicular cliffs, running as far as he could see, thrust their gray sides above the trees. The valley narrowed as tremendous lines of granite swept down to converge in a grim, twisting slash in the earth.

"There's the Saco River," Luther said, pointing. Ben was surprised to see a brook that he could have jumped across.

It chattered along in its rocky bed and disappeared from sight under the drooping branches of a gnarled old fir tree.

"You'll see plenty of it before we pull into Portland," Luther promised. "Here it's just a baby. Indians call it *Skok-kooe*. Supposed to mean something like *river that snakes through the pine trees,* though it beats me how they could pack that much into one little word."

The trail dipped downward and twisted its way deeper into the cleft. Boulders, ribs of bare rock, mudholes, and tangles of blown-down softwood made their progress a nightmare. Ben thought that terrific winds must funnel through the gorge from time to time.

The Saco came in sight again on their right. Larger already, it dashed against the jumbled mass of boulders that formed its bed as though looking for a way out.

"Ho-hish!" Luther called sharply, and as the oxen strained, Ben bent his shoulder to the high rear wheel. The wagon rumbled reluctantly up and over a granite spur. The team stood, heaving. Ben leaned on the heavy wooden hub and rubbed his hot face against his sleeve.

"I swear, I don't think you care for traveling," Luther said with a laugh. "You don't know how good the road is now. I've been told that the first man who went through the notch—fellow by the name of Nash, who discovered it—had to help his horse up and down cliffs with a rope."

Ben snorted. "Maybe it would have been just as well if he hadn't found it. Then we could have floated down the Connecticut."

"Oh, but you get blisters from the oar sweeps," Luther objected. "And the falls are fearsome." He gave Ben a sly look. "Though you, being good at swimming under water, might not mind a ducking . . ."

Ben straightened up as though he'd been bitten. He stalked around to the far side of the wagon, kicked the wheel sharply, and dislodged some clods of mud. The axles were beginning

to squeal again. He lifted the birch bucket full of grease that
swung from the wagon brace and wielded the wooden paddle
vigorously.

"Good lad," Luther said unexpectedly. He turned again to
the oxen. "Hup, Star and Buck." The wagon rumbled forward on solid rock for a few feet, then sank into deep muddy
ruts. Ben grabbed the wheel spokes again and heaved. What
must it be like coming back—uphill?

It was wild and gloomy where they stopped for their noon
meal. Ragged old spruces leaned in every direction, and some
had fallen into the river, which was now a brawling torrent.
After eating, Ben's eyes grew heavy. He roused with embarrassment when Luther called. For once a nap had caught up
with him.

When they finally made camp for the night, both of them
were too tired for talk. Luther pulled the wagon in under
an overhanging ledge, and Ben built the fire where it would
reflect off the rock. They hobbled exhaustedly around the
camp, fixing a sketchy supper. A batch of johnnycake was
set to bake on a maple chip, and salt pork was browned in
the spider. Luther brought in a handful of leeks that he had
stumbled onto while picketing the animals.

They ate silently and afterwards rolled into their blankets
almost at once. Ben wiggled his aching back on the uneven
ground and wondered with a sudden flicker of respect how
Plin took such a beating and still managed to wear a frock
coat. He probably didn't lift a finger to help Luther on the
road.

The next day was a repetition of the last, except that a
light rain fell during the morning, making the footing even
more uncertain. Once they had to stop while Luther made
a minor repair on a wagon wheel.

Finally, the valley widened out, but the way was still
bounded by grim dark slopes and the rushing Saco River.

After several hours of travel, the river and the trail turned at right angles, to the east, and Ben felt that they were at last getting somewhere. The following morning brought easier traveling. Groves of trees bordered natural meadows, with the river, now a wider but less tempestuous stream, flowing through the center.

They stopped early. While the animals grazed, Ben caught a string of fish that made good eating for supper. From their campsite under a leaning willow, he saw an occasional traveler pass. First, two carts rumbled by, driven by straw-hatted men. They were followed by a man with long, flowing hair, who rode a sway-backed roan horse. Ben thought the man said something to him, and raised himself on his elbow, but then noticed that the stranger was only reading aloud from a small book he carried. He looked questioningly at Luther.

"A preacher," Luther said. "Maybe he's practicing for his next camp meeting. Some of these traveling preachers cover a big territory. Lots of little settlements wouldn't ever hear the gospel if it wasn't for them."

"Where's he heading now?" Ben asked.

"I hear there's a crossing just north of here," Luther answered.

"You've never gone that way?"

"No. I've got troubles enough out here where it's civilized. Fellow with a pack-horse load of notions could probably find mighty fine bartering up in there, though."

"What kind of notions would a peddler take into the back country?" Ben asked.

"Oh, same things they take anywhere. Gimcracks and doodads, but not too heavy or too bulky. You've seen the goods that the peddlers bring through St. Johnsburg."

"Not much," Ben confessed. "Pa doesn't hold with fripperies. But once Ma traded a muffler she'd knit for a paper of brass pins that came from London."

"Peddlers come in two kinds," Luther observed, "gentle-

men of the road and rascals. The rascals make the most noise
and are remembered the longest. Ever hear of wooden nut-
megs and gun flints made of cow horn?"

Ben nodded.

"Well, they didn't grow out of somebody's imagination. Or
maybe they did, at that—some lazy, good-for-nothing dreamed
them up as ways to make a dishonest penny. Easier to sit by
the fire and whittle wooden spices than it is to stir around
and tan a pelt or weave a basket."

Ben poked a half-burned stick back into the fire with his
bare toes. "I've heard tell of awful dealings with peddlers,"
he said, shaking his head.

"Now hold on, boy. Don't belittle the lot. Might be a rotten apple or two in the basket, but you don't have to throw
out the whole shebang. Peddlers do a lot to make things
easier and pleasanter, especially for the womenfolk. The
gewgaws they carry are the sort of thing that can't be du-
plicated at home. Besides, a woman likes something that's not
downright necessary once in awhile. Give her a pretty shawl
and probably she lays it away, but she's humming when she
goes back to the washtub."

Ben stared in surprise at the trader. He'd never have supposed that Luther would give a woman's likes any thought.
What man could ever figure out what the silly things wanted
anyhow! Still, a trader had to be sharp, and women were
often his customers. Ben decided he'd have to think about
women a little.

Luther scratched his black thatch of hair vigorously. "Now
you take news," he said. "When we get hold of a newspaper,
what do we get? Some editorials about what Congress is
doing, a list of what the apothecary has got to sell, and a
notice that there's a new dish mill starting up—forty miles
away. The real news comes from the traveling men—peddlers
and tinkers and all the rest."

"We've had a few to the house," Ben agreed. "Ma always asks them to stay for supper."

"Sure. Women don't mind feeding an extra mouth if, in between bites, it'll tell the latest gossip from up and down the road."

Ben flopped over on his stomach. "When that shoemaker was in town last fall, all he did was talk about politics," he remarked. "He knew a lot about different candidates, and he told Pa what folks in the other towns were saying about them."

"Wouldn't wonder," Luther wheezed. "Politicians take pains to get in good with all the traveling men they can. Does office seekers no harm to have their names come up when the peddler unrolls his wares on the doorstep in some outlying clearing or maybe under a tree on the village green. *Providing* the talk is favorable."

"That cobbler said the editor in Peacham was going to help put Horace Cutler into the government. He had some copies of *The Green Mountain Patriot* that he was *giving* away. My brother Will read some of the writing. It said we have to have a bold government to weld the wild elements together."

Luther gave a snort of laughter.

"You sound like sort of a wild element, Luther," Ben said slyly.

"I guess I am kind of untamed," Luther admitted. "All that blather kind of riles me. That's why I stay away from politics."

"It said something about the country crawling with ignorant men who haven't learned to cooperate," Ben said with a grin. "Seems like the years of revolution were a bad influence, and they got into the habit of being against what's good for 'em."

Luther shifted irritably. "I was just a tad," he muttered, "but I minded the horses for some of the men in old Ike Putnam's regiment. I don't believe any of those tired men thought they were being influenced in a bad way. Sometimes it seemed there were more able-bodied men wagging their tongues down in Boston than were waving their muskets in the ranks, but some of the talkers were right in there fighting, in their way."

"If wagging a tongue is what it takes, Cutler will be President," Ben said, his tone turning bitter.

"Don't know but what it takes a mite more than that," Luther protested mildly. "Don't worry. Probably Horace wouldn't do any great harm if he did get into office."

"Well, I wouldn't vote for him if every peddler from here to Boston thought him worthy," Ben said roughly. As he flopped over on the grass, his elbow hit a freshly cleaned fish and he skidded wildly, cracking his head against a stick of firewood. "Ow!" he howled, struggling to his feet. He stamped off toward the river bank, followed by Luther's loud laughter.

X

Trouble—and a Friend

The closer the rocking wagon drew to the coast, the heavier grew the stream of travelers. With something new and exciting to see at every turn, Ben often forgot to watch his footing. Twice he walked into a wagon wheel, but he scarcely noticed his skinned shins. There were men on horseback and women in carts. Peddlers balancing bulky packs trudged by and waved cheerfully. Once a flock of sheep flowed around the wagon and pattered on with plaintive bleats. They were driven by an old man who carried one arm in a sling made by the knotted end of his long white beard.

Everywhere was the sound of the ax and saw, the creak of wheels, and the shouts of wagoners. The mountains were receding to the north and west behind them, and the road passed along land so flat that Ben marveled. They approached a stand of towering softwoods that Ben thought must be white pine. The soaring tops were breathtaking against the blue sky.

"How tall you figure they are?" Ben asked, craning his neck.

"Masting pines sometimes go to two hundred and forty

feet," Luther replied, squinting skyward. "Reckon these are two hundred, easy. See there? That white pine's got the mark of the King's broad arrow on it. It was reserved for His Majesty's Navy, but he didn't get it after all!"

Ben listened to the wind sighing through the distant crowns of the trees. The straight, tapering trunks looked to be six feet through at the bottom. He walked on quietly, feeling uncomfortably insignificant. At the rate that lumber was being hauled toward the coast, he wondered whether there would be a stick standing the next time he came this way. The road was choked with wagonloads of freshly sawed boards, carts piled with shingles, and drays full of mighty timbers. Luther drew up behind one of the loads and halted Buck and Star with a word.

Ahead of them, three span of wild-eyed, mud-splattered steers lunged spasmodically under the excited urging of their angry driver. On one side, the broad wheels of the truck, attached front and back to enormous logs, had dropped into a mudhole, and the load canted dangerously.

The big, black-bearded wagoner strode back alongside his team, shaking his goad and shouting violently in French. The teamster stretched his arms to the sky. "Jacques! Jacques!" he roared.

It was then that Ben saw an undersized, black-eyed boy standing warily by the side of the road, well out of reach of the furious driver.

"Now, see here, Joe!" Luther wheezed, clumping forward. "Let those beasts be until you've got hold of yourself."

The Frenchman turned on Luther with a scowl. Then he raised his shoulders in an exaggerated shrug. *"Eh bien!* I let stupid ox stand," he said sarcastically, "and leetle birds fly load to Portland, no?"

Luther said grimly, "If you don't get that load out of the way, the road will be jammed with lumbermen clean back to Fryeburg—every one of 'em looking for the cause of the holdup with a pike pole in his hand."

"You t'ink I don't know!" the wagoner yelled, waving his arms. "Dat mud, she's got no bottom. Eet ees no use."

"Well, I never found a hole in Vermont I couldn't bridge," Luther rasped gently, "and none in Maine up to now. Let's take a look, Joe."

"Joe—bah! I am Alphonse Jean Pierre Dufresne," the wagoner stated irritably but proudly.

Ben strolled past the bound timbers toward the boy near the edge of the road. His black hair curled tightly over the rolled-up edges of a little knit cap that perched on the back of his head, and a purple bruise stretched across one thin cheek. His jacket was ragged and his bare feet covered with mud. He kept a cautious eye on Ben.

Ben smiled and jerked his head toward the men. "Mighty soft spot," he commented. "Likely there's a spring in there."

The boy nodded vigorously. "We need help," he said. A grin lit his face. "It is good that you are big!"

Ben figured the boy must be a couple of years younger than himself. "That your father over there?"

"My *oncle*. I am Jacques Fornier."

"*Shock?*" Ben said doubtfully.

The black-haired boy slapped his thigh and laughed. "*Non, non!* Jacques."

"Z-z-yock," Ben said carefully.

"Maybe bettair you call me Shorty as the woodsmen do!"

"Ben," came Luther's cracked shout. "Take an ax and cut me a pole about twenty feet long and, say, five inches across. Can that nipper understand English?"

"Yup," Ben called back. "Seems to."

"Tell him to swamp out a place on the right bank so we can swing the lead team that way."

"*Comprenez-vous, Jacques?*" the teamster yelled. "*Allons!*"

"Oui!" Jacques said hastily and went for his ax on the run.

Ben pulled his ax off the load and made his way to a young ash that stood a little way off. As he felled the tree and then cut off its limbs with deft strokes, he could hear the sound of Jacques' ax and an occasional breathless grunt as the boy cleared away seedling pines and heaved rotting trunks of fallen trees to one side.

When he stumbled back to the road, the fresh-cut pole bumping behind him, Ben saw that Luther had unhitched Buck and Star from the wagon and goaded them into position ahead of the other teams. Jacques was working feverishly to make a space where the teams could swing wide and angle the wheels out onto the high side of the road.

They jabbed the long, limber pole hard under the buried front wheel. Ben leaped for a hold on the pole and yanked himself hand-over-hand up its length until he dangled from its top end. Jacques swarmed up nimbly and added his slight weight just below.

Luther settled his hat, braced his feet, and touched Buck's shoulder with the goad. "Easy, boys," he said. "Hup!"

Alphonse flailed his arms and boomed, "Together, you miserable goats. *Marche!*"

Obediently the heavy heads bowed. Muddy clods flew as sharp hoofs dug and flanks strained. Ben and Jacques bobbed wildly on the bending pole, as the truck creaked, moved, settled back. Alphonse snapped his whip threateningly over the backs of the teams, and both men shouted. At last, with a sucking sound, the broad wheel moved slowly upward, helped by the leverage of the pole. As the wheel lifted, the angle of the pole declined, and Ben and Jacques were slowly lowered until their feet touched the ground. They doubled over the pole then, balancing their weight on their thighs while the dray crept precariously higher.

Luther turned the steers as sharply as he could, and they fought their way up the slight bank to solid ground. The rear wheels of the long load rumbled safely past the churned hole, and men and cattle came to a panting halt.

"Aha, we have done the impossible!" Alphonse shouted, his white teeth gleaming above his black beard. *"Mon ami—*my friend*—merci. Merci beaucoup!"*

"Ayah." Luther acknowledged the thanks with a bob of his head. He began unyoking his oxen from the load. "Believe I'll just let the critters rest and eat a mite whilst we get some logs into that hole. I want to get my wagon over without going around through the woods."

"I will help you," declared Alphonse. "Jacques!"

By the time the four of them had completed a pole road over the worst of the mudhole, Ben was sweating freely and hungry enough to eat one of the oxen. He said as much to Jacques.

Jacques seemed to understand. He rubbed his flat stomach and led the way to the dray. Out of a leather bag he produced a long oval loaf of dark bread and a wheel of yellow cheese. Another dip into the bag and he brought out a glazed clay bottle. Whistling, he led the way to a fallen trunk and straddled it comfortably. Ben dropped to the ground, crushing the woolly stems of a patch of Indian paintbrush, and leaned back against the moss-covered log.

They chewed in contented silence and took deep drinks of the root beer from the clay bottle. Finally Ben squinted upward and mumbled, "You do this all the time, Jacques?"

"Non," Jacques said sadly. "Only three times each day—sometimes just two."

"I don't mean eat," Ben said crossly. "Do you and your uncle haul timber all year?"

"Oui. We are very fine teamsters. But it is much better in the snow, because with *le travois*—the sled—we draw bigger loads. Such loads!" Jacques' eyes snapped.

Across the road, Luther and Alphonse shared the contents

of Luther's provision box. Alphonse then began to hum a tune, his anger forgotten.

"*Oncle* Alphonse is love the party," Jacques said. "All night he plays the fiddle and sings. Pretty soon, we come to Saccarrappa—it is not far—where there are many Canadians. Maybe we will stop and visit."

"I didn't know we went through another place before we got to Portland," Ben said with surprise.

"*Mais oui.* Many mills are in Saccarrappa, and many woodsmen, oxen, and horses. Sailors on the big ships say the beef on the mess table is the horse that has died of old age and much work at Saccarrappa. They sing such a song."

Before long Luther got his team on the road again. Ben waved as they started off.

"I will look for you at the wharves," Jacques shouted.

Night found Ben and Luther moving in a solid stream of vehicles. The air was full of shouts and curses from tired wagoners, the screeching of ungreased axles, and the plaintive lowing of droves of weary animals. Foot travelers kept to the side of the dusty road. Pinpoints of yellow light showed that candles had been lit in wayside houses. The pack horse and the cow tied at the back of Luther's wagon bobbed along with heavy-footed awkwardness. Just behind them a fat white horse plodded between the shafts of a light two-wheeled cart. Crates of chickens and ducks were stacked high behind the hunched cart driver, and every bird seemed to have thrust its neck through the slats.

Ben, stumbling along behind the sagging Clara, turned time after time to watch the dozens of unblinking eyes, fixed apparently on him. In the growing dusk, the driver was a faceless shadow under the brim of his wide straw hat. Finally, he hailed Ben. Ben stopped and let the cart draw alongside.

"Where you aim to spend the night, Bub?"

"Don't know. Hope it's not much farther, though."

The driver nodded. "I'm a stranger around these parts, but I've heard about Broad's Tavern on the Stroudwater Road."

"I'll have to ask Luther," Ben said, and turned to find the teamster at his elbow.

"This is the Stroudwater," Luther explained, his voice more cracked than usual. "Only way to Portland Town is through this neck. I don't hold with Broad's place though. There's a roadhouse about half a mile ahead though, where they serve good soup in a big bowl."

"I'll follow along then and be obliged to you," said the stranger. "Porter's my name."

"I'm Chickering from upper Vermont," Luther replied. "Ben here is my helper."

"All the way from the Grants, eh? That must be a rough trip."

"Bad enough," Luther acknowledged. He rapped his goad on the wagon box and spoke sharply to the oxen.

XI

A Fight in the Yard

Ben was cheered when they turned into the big, noisy yard of the roadhouse. Light from the windows of the low building streamed out onto the teeming shadows, and the rich kitchen smell went straight to the pit of Ben's empty stomach. Several teamsters, late like themselves, were bawling commands and cracking whips.

They backed the wagon against the rough fence, and Porter maneuvered his cart close beside it. The animals seemed to take forever at the watering trough, and Ben was convinced that the food would be all gone before he could get inside.

Finally, when even the chickens were fed, after a fashion, Ben and the men washed up at the long bench beside the door and tramped in. The big room was rough and bare of furniture but filled with people. Teamsters of every description stood, sat, or walked about, some spooning hungrily from bowls, some drinking from tall mugs. A noisy group in one corner argued and banged the table.

At the door of the lean-to kitchen, Luther, Ben, and Porter accepted their steaming bowls gratefully. Unable to see an opening at any of the tables, they edged their way toward the corner and sat down with their backs to the wall. The fireplace was lit, more for light than for warmth, and it threw an uncertain glow over the room.

Ben's eyes were drawn to one brawny young teamster who was wearing a shirt of beautiful deep red towcloth. Beetroot dye, Ben guessed, and wondered how the owner would like it after the first time it got wet and stained his skin. Ma was forever distracted because beetroot faded so, and she used it only now and again to make something pretty for Goody.

Luther nudged Ben with his elbow and directed his attention to the boisterous group at the nearby table. "Bunch of roughnecks," he muttered.

Ben watched covertly. Certainly they looked ugly. One man seemed especially mean, with a seamed, dark face and a twisted mouth. As he tossed his head with a roaring laugh, his long greasy hair was flung back briefly, and Ben saw that an ear was missing. The table grew quiet as the men leaned forward, their heads close together. There were chuckles and whispers.

"I don't like the look of that crowd," Porter said nervously.

"They won't start anything here," Luther declared, "but I'd as leave have a stout club to hand if I met 'em alone somewhere." He took off his old hat and hung it over his bent knee, then fished out the small drawstring pouch that held his tobacco.

Suddenly the table beside them erupted in a fury of yells, crashing chairs, and violent blows. Ben leaped to his feet barely in time to avoid a heavy-booted foot that swung past his head. He struck at a blocky form that came reeling toward him, but was jerked roughly back by a hand on his own collar.

"Stand aside, sprig," Luther said flatly.

Porter was ducking in and out below the flying fists, trying to collect their bowls. An angry howl was followed by a bone-jarring thud as one of the men dropped at their feet. He made no effort to get up.

"Guess he's through," Luther said calmly. "Heft his feet."

Ben grabbed the bare ankles and struggled into the press of onlookers. They drew back enough to make a passage to the door. Luther dropped the man's shoulders roughly on the trampled ground. As he and Ben straightened, someone else deposited a second unconscious figure beside the first.

Then a tangle of bodies spewed across the doorstep, some staggering to their knees. A huge man planted himself in the doorway and surveyed the cursing, crawling trouble-makers.

"Enough of that!" he said sharply. "Don't show your faces around here again!"

"Now things'll quiet down a mite," Luther observed. "Ben, spread your blankets on the grassy patch by the fence —it's too muddy under the wagon—and I'll finish my pipe and bed down by the fire."

Ben walked slowly across to the wagon, after picking theirs out from the lumpy black bulks of loaded carts and wagons that stood everywhere. Small thumps came from the stockade as cattle and horses settled down for the night.

Two of the brawlers limped past with a black look at Ben. He felt uneasy as he lifted his blanket roll out of the wagon and squinted along the fence for a smooth-looking spot. He yawned widely. How could he ever stay awake to guard the load if he lay down? His eyelids seemed hung with weights, and he leaned against the wheel, hugging his bedding. He had no doubt that he could sleep soundly even on top of a rail fence. But what if those toughs came sneaking back to see what they could steal? After all, Luther's wagon was conveniently close to the gate. Ben turned to look down the road. Barely visible in the starlight, two dark shapes had halted and were talking together. As he watched, one straightened and waved his arm toward the roadhouse, which made Ben surer than ever that something was afoot.

He gave a great sigh of frustration. Must he spend the night walking round and round the wagon? On the other side of the yard, a few men were rolling up for the night behind high wheels. They'd probably think him daft if he started circling—and he was so sleepy. A soft breeze swept through the pines. Ben slumped against the wagon wheel, and his chin dropped slowly. Tarnation! *What* was he going to do?

A couple of the chickens in the crates on Porter's wagon clucked drowsily. Ben finally made a decision. Quickly he spread his blankets beside the fence. After that, he trotted back and forth between the wagon and the cart, then dug in his packsack for a couple of things. Some of the chickens were disturbed by the commotion and squawked irritably. A few moments later, Porter stepped to the door of the roadhouse and peered out.

"Nothing's wrong," Ben called softly.

Porter waved his hand and disappeared. Ben took a last look around, slid into his blankets, and yawned so hard that his jaws cracked. He was peacefully asleep almost before his mouth closed.

Sometime later, when the slow stars had moved to new positions behind the tasseled pines and dew sparkled dimly on the roof, Ben sighed comfortably and turned over. But even as he pulled the blanket over his shoulder, there was a sudden curse and a splintering crash almost at his side. A terrible squawking came from the crated chickens, and angry shouts and the thud of running feet added to the uproar.

The door of the roadhouse burst open, and two men dashed out in pursuit of a running, shouting trio. As he struggled to his feet, Ben saw the nimbler pair overtake the fleeing forms and bear them to the ground in yelling confusion. He rushed over to the group, where one dim figure had his hands at the throat of another and was cracking his head against the ground.

Ben reached down, grabbed, and lunged back, roughly

dragging the top man to his knees. At this, the man swore, let go his hold on the figure underneath, and threw a punch at Ben. Fortunately, his reach from the kneeling position was short, and Ben jumped back without harm.

The man abandoned his earlier foe, still prone and showing no enthusiasm for rising, and turned his attention to Ben. As the fellow scrambled to his feet, Ben recognized the knotted muscles and bright sleeves of the red-shirted teamster he had noticed at suppertime. He stepped back in confusion. Obviously the young teamster didn't recognize *him*. Ben didn't like being mistaken for a ruffian, and it didn't look as though the teamster was going to hold still for an explanation.

Just then, someone came pounding from the doorway with a lantern. Ben broke and ran toward the light, the teamster in determined pursuit.

"Belay that!" yelled the man with the lantern, and both of the runners skidded to a halt before him.

"What in tarnation is going on here?" questioned the man. Ben took him to be the proprietor.

"The toughs who made the trouble before . . ." the teamster puffed. "They came back. We caught 'em stealing chickens."

"I heard," said the proprietor grimly. "Now, me young hearty, you're caught red-handed. Had you no better sense than to come back after the warning?" He lifted the lantern and shone it into Ben's face.

Ben's heart thumped, and he swallowed angrily. "You'll not lump *me* with those bullyboys!" he said hotly. "I came here with Luther Chickering's wagon."

"Well, by the Lord Harry, you were pounding on me when I had your sneaking friend where he belonged!" The teamster made a threatening motion.

"Don't you touch me!" Ben warned. A knot of spectators

had drawn around them, and he didn't like the expressions on their faces. Where in thunder was Luther?

"We've had too many trouble-makers here," one man said grimly. "We ought to teach him and his light-fingered friends a lesson that'll make 'em all give this place a wide berth."

The crowd pressed closer, and there was a growl of agreement. Ben looked wildly at the circle of angry men. He knew they would take care of any threatening situation without hesitation. Standing in the chill night wind, the fitful gleam of the lantern lighting the hostile ring of faces, he shivered. The long miles stretching between the trampled yard in which he stood and the familiar door rock at home suddenly seemed endless.

A whoop sounded from outside the circle, and the faces turned their attention to two men who were being hustled toward the house. As they passed, Luther squeezed under the raised arm of the landlord, who still held his lantern aloft.

"Confound it, Ben, can't I turn my back without you getting everything tied into half hitches?" he grumbled.

"Well, if he's not one of 'em, why'd he land on my back?" the young teamster demanded sourly.

Ben stood silently, his stricken eyes on his employer.

"'Cause if brains were gunpowder, he wouldn't have enough to blow his nose!" Luther wheezed caustically. He put a rough hand on Ben's arm and pushed toward the wagon. "Go on, go on."

Ben clumped back to the wagon, waves of shame and frustration surging through him. He wanted to yell and kick. He stood at the wagon wheel and pounded his fist against the iron-shod rim in helpless fury.

Porter got his lantern going and hurried about, lifting and stacking the crates of chickens. "What the—what's this?" he muttered as his foot caught in a dangling cord. He raised the splintered crate that had dropped to the ground and frowned at the length of rawhide that was tied to the corner. White feathers drifted into the dark as the chickens fluttered nervously inside. He quickly wrapped the thong across the gaping end of the crate.

Luther also checked his load as carefully as he could in the uncertain light, and then walked around to give Porter a hand. He, too, was struck by the sight of a rawhide thong that hung from the tailgate of his wagon. Ben slouched glumly against the wagon body, rubbing his bruised hands. He didn't even look up when Luther shuffled to his side.

"By jingo, I believe I'm beginning to get an idea of what went on here," he said, his high-pitched voice sounding rather baffled. "Did you set a couple crates of chickens on top of our load?"

Ben nodded silently and went on rubbing his knuckles.

"And did you stretch a couple of lines between Porter's load and ours and hitch them to the crates?"

Ben nodded again, his chin still on his chest.

"Well, I swan to man," Luther said thoughfully. "So those rapscallions *did* come back. They crept through the gate and made for the nearest wagons. And just about the time they thought they had their hands on some of my pelts, their big feet got tangled up in a thong and pitched a few dozen squawking chickens into the middle of the whole shebang!"

He slapped his knee and guffawed. "Porter!" he called. "I've seen a man catch a rooster plenty of times, but I never saw a rooster catch a man before! Hee, hee, hee!"

XII

Yankee Trader

Luther's awkward caravan took to the road early the next morning under a fair sky. Ben was in such a fever of impatience by then that he would not have noticed if it had been snowing. It had seemed to take forever to snug down the load, eat a scrap of breakfast, and get under way. The roadhouse yard was a bedlam. Judging from the yells of the teamsters, Ben figured that all the oxen must be deaf.

Portland was just over the hill. Portland and the waterfront—ships from China and the West Indies, and high white houses and shops full of treasures. He had never seen the oxen move with such deliberation. In spite of the early hour, many travelers were already abroad. A merry tootling drifted ahead of a postboy, who rode proudly with his tin horn slung next to his saddle.

They passed fine farms with woodpiles stacked neatly and with orchards on the hillsides. Soon the buildings grew closer together and a church spire split the blue sky. Finally, the wagon rattled onto a narrow street that was paved with stones. The glass in dozens of windows winked in the sunshine. People passed up and down on little walks beside the street.

Now Ben felt that the oxen were hurrying unnecessarily; he
didn't have time to take in all the sights and sounds and
smells.

Luther clumped steadily forward, now and then muttering
when he was forced to swing his team to avoid other equi-
pages. Buck rolled his eyes at a basketmaker who bobbed by
with a festoon of baskets that almost hid him from view, and
Luther calmed the ox with a word.

The town was bursting with activity, and anvils clanged
and saws screeched. The smell of the sea was in the air. Gulls
swooped overhead, and beyond the rooftops, Ben caught a
glimpse of swaying masts and reefed sails.

"There must be a thousand houses!" he marveled.

"I think that's overestimating things a mite," Luther said.
"Probably five hundred, though. Everything from log shanties
to the shipowners' palaces. Portland is a real old town. French
and Indians burned it in 1690, and folks had to start over.
Then the British shelled and burned it in 1775, and they had
to begin again. Of course, back then it was called Falmouth."

Ben kept looking around as Luther went on talking.

"I heard tell that the first cargo shipped out of Portland
was a shipload of furs and sassafras root sent over to England.
Once they got started, they didn't know when to quit.
They've shipped just about anything you can think of—barrel
staves, clapboards, masts, salt fish, even scalps."

Ben trudged along with his jaw hanging slack. The wagon
clattered and creaked. Luther scratched his shoulder with the
tip of the goad, then nudged the steers to a brisker pace.

"Look at that!" Ben exclaimed.

Out of a side street came a fantastic dragon, its length
weaving back and forth on thirty pairs of legs. Ben forgot to
walk and then had to jump aside to avoid being run down
by his own wagon.

Luther nodded. "That's a ship's hawser being moved from
somebody's ropewalk." Ben watched the men disappear, blue

pantaloons flapping, heads cocked to one side of the enormous rope they carried on their shoulders.

A few minutes later, Luther swung the oxen into a busy courtyard and stopped.

"Where are we?" Ben asked, staring at the long, sagging building. A loading platform stretched along the side, and everywhere men and boys were rolling barrels and hoisting sacks and kegs.

"Well, good for you," Luther said dryly. "I wondered if you'd come around enough to ask, in case you wanted to find the place again. This is Pelham's Warehouse on India Street. I do a lot of business here. Now mind the cattle while I hunt up Josiah or one of his clerks."

Ben draped his lean length over a wagon wheel and waited. A little way along the wooden platform, a tall man was making up a pack of tinware. The gleaming pans winked in the sunlight. Ben thought how much nicer it was than the dull, dented pewter that his mother prized. He shifted his weight and wondered what was keeping Luther. The man shouldered the bulky load of cooking ware and left.

Ben drew out from the wagon the thin little pack of items he had brought along to trade for himself—a couple of butter prints he had carved last winter, the last of the pelts from his stretching frames, and some long rawhide thongs like the two he had used on the chicken crates. He had made them carefully from deerhide.

A cart pulled up in the space where the tin peddler had been, and two men jumped down from the high seat. One vaulted to the platform and disappeared inside the building. The other busied himself uncovering the load, and soon more tinware glinted in the sun. Ben marveled. It looked as though every housewife from Maine to Georgia would have tinware before long.

"Good day," said the man sociably as he caught Ben's look. He was a small man, nimble and nervous in his movements.

"Hello," Ben replied gruffly, embarrassed to have been caught staring, but still curious. "You peddling tinware, too?"

"No sir!" said the man vigorously. "I'm a tinsmith. This is a special order, bound for Philadelphia. See here, now." He turned to the wagon, picked out a bundle, and unwound the rough cloth in which it was wrapped. Inside was a small tin box like a chest. It was about twelve inches long and half as deep, and had a neat, hinged cover. But it was the color that Ben found most amazing. The whole box was painted the deepest, glossiest black imaginable. And the cover and the front were decorated with small, delicate leaves and brilliant flowers in red, blue, and yellow.

"Real Japan lacquer," the tinsmith said with satisfaction. "How do you like that, sir? Or this one?" He unwrapped another package and showed a second box, this one painted white with a riot of black, gold, and blue on the lid.

Ben swallowed. He'd give his arm to take one of those home to Ma. "I expect they're awfully dear," he said glumly.

"Well, now, I wouldn't say they're cheap," the tinsmith admitted. "Lot of fine craftsmanship there. Am I right in thinking you'd like to have one of these boxes that the ladies of Philadelphia are begging for?"

"You're right; but you're wrong if you think I've got any money," Ben said, gloomier than ever.

"Hm—that does present a problem." The tinsmith stuck out his lower lip and blinked. "Ought to be some way to get around a problem like that when good fellows put their heads together on it. How about that big load behind you? Nothing there you'd like to trade?"

"Not mine," Ben growled unhappily. "Leastwise, nothing but a few pelts and a gimcrack or two."

"Pelts, did you say? Well, any man with furs has something to his credit. Why don't you let me look 'em over?"

Ben fumbled feverishly with his pack. He spilled the whole thing on the ground and unrolled the beaver skins hopefully. One was an especially beautiful specimen, long and dark and thick. The tinsmith brushed it with the back of his hand and fingered the others briefly.

"Nice," he said approvingly. "Must have cold winters where you come from." He cleared his throat. "Well, I'll probably lose out on this trade, but I don't like to see you disappointed. Want to swap even? Which box do you like best?"

"The black one," Ben said without hesitation. He was beaming as he took it carefully in his hands. Nothing like this had ever been seen in St. Johnsbury! Just wait until Ma showed it to Mrs. Johnson. He wrapped it again in the cloth and stowed it with what remained of his trade goods. Portland was a wonderful town!

Luther and the tinsmith's companion came out onto the loading platform together, and Luther called to Ben.

"Back the wagon in and we'll unload."

They worked together to tug the merchandise out of the wagon. It made quite a respectable pile on the platform, Ben thought, as he straightened his aching back. Small, hooped pails of maple sugar, kegs of salt pork, bales of skins, and the ever-important potash that the woolen mills of England were so eager to receive.

"Now bring the tally book," Luther said, "and we'll see." A clerk in a ruffled shirt and paper cuffs stepped out to the platform with his lead stick ready.

Ben was hard put to it to add up the kegs and pails to match the list. He came up one short on the pork and had to count over. The clerk waited with a bored expression and finally jotted down the total with a businesslike flourish. Everything seemed to have come through in good shape in spite of the jogging and bouncing. Ben was pretty confused by the rest of the transaction, but Luther seemed to be able to keep Amaziah's goods separate from the ones he had picked up in Danville.

Seated at a table in the dark little counting room, Luther penned items in his book and added pounds and shillings, all the time scowling and muttering. He gave the clerk a rough idea of what he wanted in exchange merchandise for the trip home, and Ben was suddenly filled with apprehension that they would load up and turn back for the mountains at once. He hadn't been to the waterfront—he hadn't even seen the shops. He still had to trade his butter stamps and buy some shoes and . . .

Ben had tucked his pack under his bedroll, and Luther hadn't even noticed that he had neglected to turn in his furs. "Luther," he gasped in panic, giving the burly man's sleeve a jerk. "We're going down to the ships, aren't we? I've been thinking of those ships all the way from the Connecticut!"

"Now don't get yourself excited," Luther advised. "When I was talking to Josiah, he told me Cap'n Dow is on his way down from Boston with his coasting schooner, and Amaziah's last order is aboard her. We're going to have to wait for the *Roxie A.* or go home without salt, so we'll wait. The steers have to get some rest anyhow, and don't forget we have to get rid of the pack animals."

Ben was quiet and embarrassed as they clattered out into the street again. He remembered that if Plin had been along, he would have been doing the book work for Luther. He wouldn't have been puling like a baby to go and see the sights, either. Ben sneaked a look at Luther's face and decided the trader looked a little more grim than usual. Ben sighed and scuffed along in his broken moccasins. They weren't even headed toward the waterfront.

Luther offered no explanation, but before long he goaded the oxen into a side lane. They drew up before a tall, narrow house with a tiny window in its pointed gable and with

patches of faded red paint peeling from the clapboards. As
Luther mounted the steps, the door opened and a young
sailor in a short jacket and swinging pigtail jogged past him
down to the street.

Before Luther could lift the iron knocker, a tall, angular
woman appeared in the doorway. Her mouth was pressed
into a severe line, and her snapping black eyes looked anything but happy with what they surveyed. Luther, however,
seemed untroubled by her disapproving gaze.

"Got a room for a pair of wayfarers, Mother Greene?" he
wheezed, peering up from under the brim of his hat.

"Tramps is more like it," the woman said with a sniff.
"Happens I do." Her eyes glinted at Ben. "That's a new one,
I'm bound," she stated in a tone that allowed no argument.

"Ayah," Luther answered meekly. "Plin, poor soul, broke
his leg on the last trip out."

"Hah!" Mother Greene snorted. "A pity, no doubt, but
won't make me miss that sneaky-eyed rascal a bit more."

Ben almost smiled. Mother Greene sounded like a fine
woman.

"Well, go on, go on!" she snapped impatiently. "I can't
stand here jawing when I got pudding to make, and that
Libby's not worth a row of beans unless I stand right over
her. Get around to the back, and maybe I can scare up some
scraps to feed you on."

"Yes, ma'am," Luther said obediently and clumped back
to the wagon. As they creaked down the alley to the tiny
back yard, he muttered, "Poor Libby."

Libby turned out to be a mouselike bound girl in a ragged
skirt. In just one of her cheeks she had a pretty dimple. She
was busy taking dishes out of a cupboard as they entered the
kitchen. Although Mother Greene never stopped fussing at
the girl, Ben soon noticed that the woman took over the
harder tasks herself.

Ben admired the muscles that showed below the landlady's rolled-up sleeves. A widow woman, Mother Greene was obviously used to fending for herself at the woodpile and in the cowshed. Before they ate, Ben and Luther climbed the steep stairs to a dark box of a room high above the street. Ben's pack rattled as he lowered it, and he looked quickly to see if Luther had noticed. He wanted to show the trader his beautiful box, but for some reason he hesitated. Maybe Luther wouldn't think he'd made much of a swap, since the deal meant he had practically nothing of his own left to trade. Ben shook off his moment of doubt. What if he had no money or trade goods—right outside his window was Portland Town, and waiting for him just beyond were the long gray wharves.

Mother Greene set out plates of the morning's leftover cornmeal mush, sliced and fried brown. Ben dribbled molasses over his slices and fell to with enthusiasm. He had finished his meal long before Luther shoved back his chair, because he was so anxious to get started for the pier. He waited on pins and needles while Luther selected a splinter from the wood beside the blackened fireplace and settled back to pick his teeth with it. Ben fidgeted and fumed while Mother Greene and the trader exchanged views on the unpredictable weather, the high cost of living, and the deterioration of the world in general. They agreed that the present mad pace, with sailing ships dashing across the seas and stage lines tearing around the land, would bring about the ruination of decent living.

Ben sprawled in his chair and stared dolefully at poor Libby until she became flustered and dropped a plate. Finally, Luther heaved himself to his feet and allowed that they ought to be getting down to Fore Street.

"Can I find a trade there?" Ben asked as he jumped eagerly to his feet.

"I'll point you to the wood market," Luther assured him. "Everything's cheaper there and trade is brisk."

"Wait while I fetch my pack." Ben sprinted up the stairs and started to take the painted box out of his sack. Then, on a sudden notion, he decided to take it with him. What if someone—Libby, maybe—should see it while he was gone and steal it? And, anyway, maybe he'd run into Jacques and he could show it to him. Ben was so proud of his treasure that he was aching to show it to someone.

As they made their way on foot toward the business section of town, Ben was more and more amazed at the activities around him. Painted signs swung over the streets, announcing counting houses, eating places, outfitters, and tradesmen of all kinds. Ben stared at the displays of navigating instruments in the windows of ship chandlers, and eyed the stores filled with china, cutlery, and clocks.

"Lots of the signs have pictures that show what the shop is selling," Ben commented.

"Have to," Luther rasped. "A lot of folks can't read too well, but their money's just as good as anybody's. And suppose you were from some foreign place—Spain or the like— how could you make out with nothing to guide you but strange words on a swinging board?"

As Luther was speaking, Ben saw a tall brown man with queerly cut clothes and a bright sash about his waist mount the stone steps and disappear into one of the buildings. Ben wondered if he was from the East Indies. Shortly afterward, a mounted couple rode by, the horses' shod hoofs ringing on the stones. The young man wore a tail coat and shining boots. His companion sat her sidesaddle gracefully, the feather in her hat nodding, but Ben wondered how on earth she kept from falling off.

Suddenly they were on Fore Street, and Ben became aware of a whirl of activity. Directly over the street hung the booms of square-riggers, and from their holds came a rocking stream of cargo on the backs of singing Negro stevedores. Overseers shouted, teamsters yelled, rigging creaked, and heavy wheels rumbled. The salt air was laced with the smells of molasses, China tea, tar, new lumber, cinnamon bark, and fish.

Overhead, tall masts swayed to the rhythm of the waves, and along the wharves, bearded sailors still swayed to the same rhythm as they walked. Ben, wide-eyed, stumbled along the paving stones. Luther glanced at him with amusement.

"Well, there 'tis," he said, "but I don't hear you say much."

"I see it," Ben mumbled. "I just haven't had time to sort it out."

"Sure a lot of goods going and coming," Luther commented. "Quite a thing when the whole world can exchange its wealth. When old Grannie Jewett's potash ends up in a London tailor shop, and Arad Weaver's salt pork goes off to the West Indies, it makes anybody stop and think. No limit to what we'll be transporting if France and England will quit quarreling and give our ships a chance."

Ben stepped to one side to avoid a team that was straining against the weight of an enormous load of shingles. A messenger boy brushed against him and gave him an impudent look as he scooted past, but Ben hardly noticed. So intent was he on the uproar around the ships that he failed to hear the fast clip-clop of hoofs coming up behind him—until a sudden screech startled him into a flying leap.

He landed awkwardly on the street and twisted around angrily to see what had bumped him. A bay horse hitched to some sort of light buggy had come to a halt just beyond, and two pretty, feminine faces were turned back toward him. The older one registered indignation, but the younger looked concerned.

"Haven't you any wits about you, young man?" asked the woman sharply. She fluttered her hand nervously. "Are you all right?"

The little girl gave her bonneted companion a quick glance. "You *were* driving rather fast, Mama," she said primly.

Ben scrambled quickly to his feet, feeling like six kinds of fool. He nodded his head vigorously and bent to dust his breeches. It was then that he caught sight of his pack, tumbled helter-skelter in the street, and the painted box was up-ended against the stones.

Ben gasped and lunged to pick it up. The little girl suddenly squealed, "Mama, Mama, see! See what he's got. Oh, I want to look at it. Make him show it to me."

Ben looked up with a frown on his face.

"Now, Annie," warned the lady.

Annie redoubled her efforts. "I want to hold it! Mama, it's the prettiest box I've ever seen. Let me, let me!" she screamed.

Her mother hung onto the reins and at the same time tried to quiet her daughter who was bouncing wildly on the seat.

"Mama, make him let me hold it!"

Ben was horribly embarrassed, for people on all sides were beginning to be attracted to the noise. He strode quickly to the buggy and passed the box to the small, outstretched hands. What sort of little wildcat was she? One yip like that from Goody, and Ma would have shut her up proper.

"Ooh!" cooed the little girl, cuddling the box. "It's so pretty."

"It is," her mother agreed, as she bent her head to examine the decorated cover.

Ben couldn't help feeling proud. Naturally everyone would like it.

"Oh, Mama, I want it!" Annie cried suddenly. She hugged the box tightly to her chest. "Won't the boy give it to me?"

"Don't be silly, child," her mother said crossly.

Ben echoed her words silently. What an idea!

"Silas gave me his silk scarf when I wanted it," Annie pouted.

"Well, that's different," her mother said impatiently. "Silas meant to fetch you something when he came back from China anyway."

"But I want it!" Annie began to sniffle. "I want to keep Miss Mary's clothes in it. *He* doesn't need it."

Ben shuffled his feet uneasily.

"It's not for doll's clothes," said her mother nervously. "Now come, dear, don't cry. Give the box back to the boy, and we'll find something nice in the shops."

For answer, Annie opened her mouth until it was nearly square and let out a howl that Ben figured could be heard back at Mother Greene's. The horse jumped and started to move ahead. Ben leaped forward, but Luther materialized from somewhere and grabbed its bridle. Annie's mother's hat was jerked over her eyes, and she gave a little scream, half in fright and half in anger. Annie, however, just kept clutching the box and went on yowling.

The woman dropped the reins and pushed back her bonnet. "Annie, you stop this minute!" she commanded in a quivering voice.

"No!" roared the little girl.

"Great heavens!" the woman said distractedly. She glanced around, then fumbled with the drawstrings of a little bag. "Here, young man!" she said with shrill insistence. She extended her arm imperiously toward Ben.

He lifted his hand automatically and felt cool metal settle heavily in his palm. Dazed, he watched Annie's tear-stained face split in a wide smile as the buggy rolled away.

The box. They had taken his box! Too late, Ben tried to protest. "Wait!" he yelled as he started to run after the buggy. Luther's solid bulk blocked his way.

"Hold on, sprout," Luther said roughly. "Reckon this little fuss is finished."

"But you saw them!" Ben yelled.

"I saw. Now you simmer down and see what she gave you."

Ben opened his fist and saw the gleam of heavy silver coins. "Money," he said dazedly, his mind still numb with the loss of his prize.

Luther looked at Ben's dejected face and made an exasperated noise. "I don't know but what it is," he said sarcastically. Then he sighed. *"Look* at it, you young idiot. Those are crown pieces. I don't know how you came by that painted chest, but what you've got in your hand would buy ten of 'em."

"I swapped my pelts for it," Ben mumbled. "The man was going to send it to Philadelphia with the rest, but he let me have it."

"Did he now?" Luther asked thoughtfully. He pushed back his disreputable hat and scratched his head. "I swear," he added, "for somebody as dumb as Adam's ox, you have the most amazing luck. First you're hornswoggled out of your furs, then you're nigh run down, and you end up with three times the money you'd have had in a fair trade for the pelts."

Ben began to liven up a little. He was pretty vague as to the value of his windfall, but Luther seemed to think it was pretty good. Probably enough to buy some shoes and breeches and a trinket for Ma to take the place of the box. And he'd have to get something for Goody. He frowned again. Nothing he could buy Ma would come close to equaling that black box. Ben's eyes dropped to the coins in his hand. He sighed.

"Come on," Luther said. "I'll show you the beginning of Back Street. The wood market lies along the east side, and there's plenty of trading going on there. I can't bear to watch you, though. Likely you'll end up buying a dozen gold-plated toothpicks. Beat it back to Mother Greene's when you're ready, but don't tarry on the waterfront after dark. I'm going now to sell the pack animals."

XIII

New Breeches

Ben was soon lost in the noisy confusion of Back Street. He wandered happily along, elbowing past knots of people, dodging teams, looking at the merchandise. He felt more at ease here. The street was crowded with farmers, tanners, and blacksmiths, and the familiar twanging speech of the northern settlements rose and fell all around him. He stopped to listen to a tall man in a tailcoat who was thundering forth on the merits of "Pettybone's Elixir, a remedy for the ills to which frail man is subject."

Bouncing on the tailboard of his painted wagon, the huckster pointed his finger dramatically at someone in the shifting crowd before him and said in a voice of doom, "Little do we know the day or the hour when calamity will strike; when sickness will fell the strong. Are *you* prepared? Do you have a supply of Pettybone's Elixir ready to do its work, ready to help you take up your burden again? No? Then *step* right up here—no crowding please—don't let this golden opportunity escape . . ."

There was a small shuffling of the group of men, and a disheveled figure ducked out in front of Ben. The boy straightened and yanked down his jacket with an explosive word of annoyance.

"Jacques!" Ben exclaimed delightedly.

"Ah. It is Ben!"

"Luther allowed I should look around here," Ben explained. "Wait till I show you . . ."

"Come away," Jacques interrupted, jerking his head toward the huckster so sharply that the ridiculous little knit cap nearly toppled from his shock of black hair. "I have only barely escaped. When he point his finger—brrr."

"We don't need his pesky tonic," Ben said with satisfaction. He threw back his shoulders and swelled out his chest.

"That medicine, it is no good," Jacques commented as they sauntered along. "*Ma tante* brews tea for the aches of the stomach, but it tastes terrible."

"So does Ma." Ben's eyes met Jacques' with complete understanding. "By jingo, I still haven't told you . . ." He fished in his jacket pocket and brought out a clinking handful of silver. "Look!"

Jacques' eyes bulged; then he looked worried. "Put it away," he whispered, frowning. "Someone will see."

"Why not? That's what's going to buy me some shoes."

Jacques peered apprehensively left and right. "But did you not—ah—find it?"

"Not so's you'd notice!" Ben said proudly. "I dickered for it."

"My friend, you are one great trader!" Jacques said admiringly. "Did you say you wish to buy the shoes? I know the place. Come, for the cobbler must hurry to have them ready before you leave."

"We can't leave for awhile," Ben explained as they picked their way down the rough street. "We're waiting for some sloop that's coming up from Boston. We took a room at Mother Greene's."

"It is mostly the coastal trade in the summer," Jacques

told his friend. "The West Indiamen stay in port through the summer. It is then that there is much trouble in the islands with fever, great winds—the hurricane, it is called—and pirates, too."

Ben's eyes shone. "Someday I'm going there," he declared. "Don't you want to go?"

"Mais, non," Jacques denied firmly, his eyes snapping. "I will have the long canoe and the paddle. Salt water—bah! So—here is the shop."

The door of the cobbler shop opened directly onto a flight of steps leading down to a dim room below the street level.

"'Allo, Gus," Jacques said cheerfully to the apron-swathed man who straddled the cobbler's bench. "We must have at once a pair of your finest shoes."

The gray-haired man smiled. "Must you now!" he said, rising stiffly. "Well, then, sit down so that I can get your measure."

"Oh, no," Jacques protested, glancing at his bare feet. "It is my friend here, the trader, who wishes shoes." He drew up his thin shoulders in a great disdainful shrug. "For shoes I have not the need," he said with dignity. "I am the woodsman, and, like the fox, I go swift and quiet. Why would I clump in shoes like a horse, eh?"

"My mistake," the cobbler said gently. "All right, Mr.—"

"Ben Tanner."

"Yes, yes, Mr. Tanner. Please sit down."

Mr. Ben Tanner, the trader, sat down. In a few minutes his shoe size had been determined, the pre-stitched cowhide uppers chosen, and the cobbler had promised to have the shoes ready the next day. Ben produced with a flourish one of his pieces of silver, but the cobbler waved the money away.

"Tomorrow," he said.

Ben sprang up the steps, feeling well pleased with himself. Out in the sunshine again, the boys hesitated. "I wonder—

what could I do about some breeches?" Ben asked. "There's not enough time to get a pair made, but I'm afraid these won't make it all the way back home."

Jacques frowned at the stained, cracked buckskins. "They are not good," he admitted. "I do not know how . . . Unless . . . Ah, I have it." He flung out his arms, and started off at a trot.

Laughing at the antics of his friend, Ben followed him through town, passing once through a narrow, bad-smelling alley where gaunt cats glared at their approach. Everywhere Ben came upon new wonders, which Jacques happily explained with much waving of arms and twitching of eyebrows. Along their way was an ink-stained printer's devil setting type in the window of the newspaper building; a sign, pointing out the office of a physician; a market where plucked chickens swung by their feet and fruit was displayed inside the doorway.

Ben wondered if any of the chickens had been his companions of the night before, but Jacques did not think so. "The live ones, they go on board ship in the coop. They sail until the cook wishes to cook. The dead chickens, they must be eaten quick or . . ." Jacques held his nose.

Ben laughed again. "What are those?" he asked, pointing to a big bundle of yellow things strung together and hanging in the window.

"Where? You mean the bananas?"

"Well, maybe. What's bananas?"

"But of course," Jacques exclaimed, "I forget that you are from the mountain country far inland. If you wish to spend a small amount, I will show you about bananas."

Ben did not hesitate. Together they stepped into the store and examined the heavy bundle. "See, they are attached to the stalk, and I have heard from the sailors how in the Indies they grow with the fingers pointing upward," Jacques explained.

Ben marveled.

"Two, my good man," Jacques stated with haughty assurance to the storekeeper. Ben nudged him and whispered, "Three."

The storekeeper told them the price, still holding firmly to the fruit that he had cut down.

Ben produced a crown, received his change, and Jacques accepted the fruit with gracious condescension. He passed two of the bananas to Ben, then split the smooth yellow side of the remaining one and peeled back a strip of skin. Ben was surprised. They weren't eaten like an apple, then. Quickly he tucked one banana into his jacket and followed Jacques' example with the other. He would save the extra one for Goody.

Munching, they walked on. Ben wondered what Tim would think if he could see him now—Tanner, the trader, eating strange tropical fruit and doing business in Portland!

They stopped to make one more purchase before they arrived at the tailor shop. On the corner, a small man was hawking something from a cart. Great bristly bundles stuck out from the cart's end, and even Jacques was uncertain what they were.

"Brooms here. Hey, new brooms," called the sad-looking huckster with little enthusiasm. It was obvious that he did not regard the two ragged boys as potential customers. They were curious, however, and stopped to finger the goods. They were straight poles, around which bundles of fine stiff straw had been bound. The boys had never seen the like, and said so.

"Made from the new broom corn," said the huckster dejectedly. "Grown last year for the first time. Nothing can beat 'em. Womenfolks won't go back to using splint brooms or hemlock once they've swept the hearth with one of these." He sighed dismally.

The boys exchanged amused glances. Jacques' eye were

dancing, and Ben was trying not to grin, for they had never before seen such a doleful peddler.

"How is business?" inquired Jacques with exaggerated concern.

"Terrible," groaned the man. "These new-fangled things will never catch on. My employer is a crazy man. I don't dare bring back any unsold, and I can't sell 'em."

"We will help you," declared Jacques. "Me and my friend, we are unexcelled peddlers of brooms—eh, Ben?" He grabbed a broom in each hand and danced out into the street. A tall grim-faced woman was crossing, her long black skirts snapping about her ankles. Jacques blocked her way, waving the brooms.

"Stop, Madam!" Jacques cried gaily. "You have not yet had the opportunity of buying one of these so magnificent brooms? *Eh bien*. Here is your broom."

She grasped the bushy thing instinctively as he thrust it toward her, then stiffened and gasped with indignation.

"Well, I never!" she exclaimed. She glared at the broom she was holding, then seized the handle capably with both hands and brought it down smartly on Jacques' shoulder.

Jacques ran for the cart, his arms crossed above his head. The angry housewife followed, diligently belaboring his bent back with the broom.

Ben doubled up with laughter, while the peddler hopped helplessly from one foot to the other and moaned despairingly. Jacques crawled under the cart and peered apprehensively from between the spokes of the wheel. The belligerent housewife handed the broom to the peddler, gave a disapproving sniff, and started to leave. Then she turned back and regarded the broom with a critical eye.

"What is the price of your brooms?" she snapped.

"One and six," gulped the huckster.

"Pshaw," she exclaimed disapprovingly. "I'll give you a pistareen." She dug a coin from her pocket, took the broom in her hand again, and with a last chilling glance directed at the cart wheel, she took herself off. The set of her shoulders suggested that she had tidied up the situation exactly to her liking.

Jacques came cautiously out from under the cart. "See, I have made the sale!" he said grandly, setting his knitted cap more firmly on his curly hair.

"I want a broom, too," Ben announced. He had decided that it would be just the present for Ma. He carefully picked a shilling from his collection of coins and pressed it into the peddler's limp hand. As the boys moved off, he slumped against the cart, his expression still hopelessly despondent.

"I don't think he appreciates our help," Jacques muttered wickedly.

Ben chuckled. "I thought that woman was going to march you off to jail or the stocks or something."

"Do not speak of jail," Jacques said, with a mock shiver. "It is better not to become involved with the jail here. It is very cold and has crawling things. Sometimes it is crowded and noisy. If you are lucky, you find a place to sleep on the planks, but without blankets. And the food—it is better to go hungry."

"How do you know?" Ben asked. "Have you been there?"

"*Non, non!*" Jacques retorted. "I am careful to stay away. It is not good to cross the law in Portland if you are French." He looked around cautiously. "The French Revolution, it scare the merchants and shipowners. In private they say among themselves that the common people will rise and chop off their heads if they are not kept under control. Can you see in your mind *la guillotine* in Portland? Bah!"

"Aw—you're making sport of me."

"*Non,*" Jacques said sadly. "But soon things will be better. Soon *Oncle* Alphonse will be the citizen and be able to vote. Then he will help to elect Mr. Thomas Jefferson to be President."

"How do you know so much?"

"Ah, I talk to sailors and I listen. Along the waterfront you learn much. That also is where I learn about the jail. When sailors lose all their money or if they say too much against the British embargo and the impression of seamen, there they must go."

"Say, what kind of money is a pistareen?" Ben inquired.

"Look in your pocket. When we buy the bananas, you get one in change."

Ben shuffled his coins again.

"There," Jacques said. "It is Spanish, see? There is much Spanish money here. You have also two bits. Spanish dollars can be divided into halves and again into quarters—eight bits in all. So! Spanish coins are called pieces of eight."

"Oh," Ben said uncertainly. For a moment he felt alarmed. How could he ever be a successful trader if he couldn't keep his money straight?

"The pistareen," Jacques continued, "is—say, half a shilling. You see?"

"Clear as mud," Ben said ruefully.

Jacques wasn't listening anyway. *"Voilà!"* he shouted. "The shop of the tailor, M'sieur Grimes."

"Grimes?"

"Oui. His shop is of the best. Very grand men come here—ships' officers, merchants, lawyers. Myself, I have nevair been inside."

"Grimes," Ben repeated.

Jacques looked at him with some surprise. "Something?" he inquired.

"Oh, no," Ben said hastily. It was ridiculous to think that it would be the store of the portly traveler he had met at Alphy's inn the first night of his trip. The shop was prosperous-looking—the windows were large and clear, and hitching posts had been planted outside for the convenience of the customers.

Ben became a little anxious. "Let's go in," he said. He was afraid that if they dallied, he might lose his nerve.

The tailor shop smelled of wool and fuller's earth and steam. At one side, two tailors sat cross-legged, plying their needles. A stooped, shirt-sleeved clerk came toward the boys as they hesitated inside the door.

"Deliveries are made at the back," he stated witheringly. Ben was suddenly conscious of the broom he carried.

"We do not deliver," Jacques said with equal disdain. "We wish to purchase the breeches."

As the clerk looked them up and down, Ben was fascinated to find that he had a crossed eye. What kind of a seam did he sew? Ben wondered.

"I'm afraid you have the wrong establishment," the clerk said, looking at them contemptuously.

"Mais non," Jacques corrected him gently. "My friend has come here with purpose. He is a busy man and must leave at once for the north. There is no time to be lost."

"Well, he can't leave too soon to suit me," the clerk said, and turned on his heel.

"Just a minute," Ben said roughly. He shoved the broom forward a little and was rewarded by the sight of the haughty clerk sprawling beneath a table of fabrics. A small titter sounded from the tailors' corner.

"You tripped me!" said the clerk menacingly as he scrambled to his feet. His long, spidery fingers twisted the measuring tape that hung from his neck.

"You weren't paying attention," Ben told him. "Now, listen! I've got all the money you'll ever want for a pair of breeches. What are you going to do about it?"

The clerk seemed to be studying Ben's calloused brown fists. "Well, I'm sure I don't know what Mr. Grimes would say," he muttered indignantly. "But if you insist . . ." He yanked the tape free from his neck.

"There is one problem," Jacques put in smoothly. "Mr.

Tanner must leave Portland at once—unhappily there is not time for sewing. It is our thought that the breeches of M'sieur Jacob Jones would make the fit."

Ben glanced in surprise at his audacious friend. The thin boy winked at him and went on with composure. "Is it not true that the brig *Olive* is even now held by the French for trying to run their blockade in the West Indies? Jacob Jones and all the crew languish in the prison ship, *non?* So of what use are the breeches that he ordered, eh?"

"I see," said the clerk thoughtfully.

"At what time will Jacob Jones return for his breeches?" Jacques asked dramatically. "Perhaps nevair! The fevers, the flogging—you would do well to rid yourself of the breeches while you can."

"I'll fetch them," the clerk said abruptly.

"What's that all about?" Ben asked Jacques in a whisper.

"The *Olive* carried the lumber to Martinique. We bring the load to the pier. We help to stack it on deck, and I talk to Jacob Jones. He is young, but he has been to sea since he is twelve. He has much money, and he boasts to me that he has ordered the breeches from the best tailor in town."

Jacques shrugged and tilted his curly head. "If he comes back, he will no longer have the money. He will be glad to have his life."

While the tailor watched disapprovingly, Ben thrust his long legs into the breeches that had been laid away for Jacob Jones. They were, indeed, a good fit, except that the waist must be taken in just a little. Ben ran his hand over the blue wool, thinking that even Horace Cutler's fine feathers couldn't match this. Ben again wondered fleetingly whether the traveling Mr. Grimes could be connected in any way with the shop in which he stood.

"We'll have them altered and ready for you tomorrow," the clerk said ungraciously.

"Much obliged," Ben said. He climbed back into his old breeches.

A door slammed somewhere, and one of the tailors rose hastily and went to the door that opened into the back room. "Glad to see you back, sir," he said. Ben heard a heavy voice with a note of irritation in it, but the reply was indistinct.

The clerk cleared his throat. "That will be six shillings. It's customary for *gentlemen* to make an advance payment," he added disagreeably.

Ben slammed a crown piece down on the table and turned angrily away. That clerk certainly was looking for trouble. He picked up his broom, flung open the door, and stalked out. As the clerk scuttled to close the door, Ben saw over his shoulder a glimpse of a rotund man emerging from the back room. It was without doubt the Mr. Grimes who had tiptoed into his sleeping chamber at the inn.

XIV

Riot in the Streets

---◆---◈◉◈---◆---

"Ben, I am not sure I have done right," Jacques said in a troubled voice, as he lead the way across the street.

"Hmm?" Ben was trying to recall Grimes' actions in the inn chamber.

"That is too much money for a pair of breeches," Jacques declared. "You will have nothing left in your pocket."

Ben forgot about the tailor. "Hey, don't you worry," he said. "I want those breeches. I vow I won't go back home looking like something the cat dragged in."

"Oh, you will be the grand one!" Jacques declared enthusiastically, forgetting his qualms. "Now I must go back and find my uncle or he will use the stick on me instead of the oxen. Come to the end of the street with me. Then walk to the west and you will see the house of Mother Greene."

The sun was getting low, and as the boys approached the corner, they saw that a crowd had gathered about the steps of a sail loft. The tone of the gathering was anything but idle. Most of the men were listening intently to an argument going on between a well-dressed, top-hatted man and a gray-haired man in shirt sleeves.

"If the ports are closed, how will we live? I tell you, we must protect ourselves. Let Britain and France destroy one another if they are bent on it."

"Yes!" agreed another voice. "Let our armed merchantmen and fine new frigates move against the murdering Jacobins. Open the ports and end the rule of the bloody, ignorant masses!"

"Oh, don't talk foolishness!" cried the shirt-sleeved man as he walked nervously up to the top step. "Are there not enough hotheads in Philadelphia? They can think of no solution to any situation except war. Has not enough of the blood of our finest and best been spilled in the recent past to surfeit their bloodthirsty appetites?"

"Oh, get down!" cried someone roughly. "We've listened to your ilk long enough. What has it got us? Our sons and brothers rotting in prison hulks, Talleyrand bribing our government emissaries, our skippers tortured into admitting they carry English-owned contraband. Are we going to do nothing?"

Soon, more workmen joined the crowd, pressing those in the inner ring closer.

"Are you blind?" pleaded the man on the step. "Hardly yesterday you howled for war against the British. They were holding forts in our west; they were seizing American goods in foreign ports; they were fighting the gallant ally of our own struggle for independence—France! *Our honor is at stake,* we cried. We must free ourselves of this intolerable oppression.

"Fah! We did not fight. President Adams and his statesmen kept the peace in spite of Hamilton and his war hawks. Bitterness and humiliation we knew—but not war!"

"Get him down from there," shouted a new voice from the edge of the crowd. "We've got laws now that will take care of treacherous people who seek to pull down our government! Let the Sedition Law take care of him."

The crowd turned toward the newcomer, and there was a menacing mutter. Ben and Jacques were frozen against the wall.

"Yes, we have laws!" the man on the step thundered, speaking now to the upturned faces of the crowd. "What kind of laws? Laws that virtually abolish the Bill of Rights. What has become of those safeguards against the stifling of free speech and the press? Nullified! I'll tell you what we have—the same throats shouting for war! Again for the sake of our honor—again for the preservation of our freedom. And who is the supposed oppressor this time? Why, our gallant ally, our democratic champion—France!"

"You're right." "That's telling 'em!" the crowd shouted.

"You'd better quiet down," said the top-hatted man grimly, "or the sheriff will have you for inciting to riot, as well as for all the other things you've provoked him with."

"Keep quiet when all we fought for as young men is being swallowed up?" demanded the gray-haired man passionately. "Keep quiet when we're being treated like aliens in our own land? How . . ."

The sudden sound of thudding feet drew the listeners' attention away from the debate. A muffled curse exploded at the edge of the crowd, and then everything was a bedlam of yells and thumps and waving arms.

"It's the sheriff's men," Jacques whispered, cowering against the wall.

The hand-to-hand fighting surged nearer, and one of the sheriff's men was laying about solidly with his stave. A dark figure collapsed with a groan, then raised itself and shouted a stream of angry French.

Jacques gasped. "It is *Oncle* Alphonse!" he screamed and darted forward. Just as he got near his uncle, however, one of the officials picked up the fallen man roughly and shoved him into the little group that was being led away.

As he pounded along the pavement behind Jacques, Ben

heard him call his uncle's name, saw the swift blow that staggered Jacques and the push that sent him reeling into the huddled bunch of men.

Ben slowed to a stop. The street had gone gray and colorless. The sun was down, and the little window panes looked blankly onto the littered road.

As Ben was berating himself for his delay in following Jacques, a man came out from behind a building and stopped beside him. "Lucky you came along late," he commented. "Were you planning to dust off the sheriff with that?"

Ben saw with dull surprise that he still carried the broom. "Oh—my mother's," he said vaguely. Then he gestured toward the little knot of men marching unevenly out of sight down the street. "Where are they going?"

"Jail," the man said, and passed on across the street.

Ben stood alone in a strange and violent place. Listlessly he started toward the boarding house. "The jail, it is very bad," Jacques had said. "The food—the crawling things . . ."

Out of the corner of his eyes, Ben saw something lying in the street. With sudden recognition he turned, scooped up Jacques' small blue stocking cap, and jammed it into his pocket. He wondered what he could possibly do to help?

Mother Greene's kitchen was hot and smoky. The joint of beef turning before the fire dripped fat into the flames, and the kettle beside it steamed briskly. Ben went on out to the tiny back yard. Luther hadn't returned, but Ben wondered if he could expect any help from Luther anyhow. The trader was awfully businesslike, and Ben hadn't done a whole lot to build up his own stature as a businessman—at least not in Luther's eyes. Probably he would squeal like a pig caught in a fence if Ben suggested they go to the jail and try to do something for Jacques and his uncle.

Disconsolately Ben wandered past the cowshed, skirted the big wooden washtubs, and ducked under the clothesline.

Against the fence was a little strip of garden vegetables. Half a dozen rows of young plants looked unexpectedly fresh and green with so much town all around. Ben dropped to his knees, pulled a couple of weeds out of the onions, and began to feel more at home. The dirt was different here, though—heavy and sticky. He worked until Luther spoke from the kitchen door.

"So there you be. Come in before Libby eats all the beef."

Ben jumped to his feet, splashed water on his stained hands, and hurried up the steps. As they ate, Libby hovered in the background, ready to pour tea or fork more greens onto their plates.

"How'd you make out by yourself?" Luther inquired. "At least you're not in jail."

"No, *I'm* not, but . . ." Ben took a quick look at Mother Greene's face and decided she might be an ally. He poured out the story of his meeting with Jacques and the shocking way that the afternoon had ended. "We've got to do something!" he said fiercely.

Luther and Mother Greene snorted in unison. "You don't know what you're saying, boy," Luther told him reprovingly. "Best not meddle in anybody's affairs, and *never* in the sheriff's."

"What kind of freedom is it when a man can't open his mouth without getting arrested!" Ben said indignantly.

"Now see here," Luther said gruffly, "the sheriff acted according to his lights. They're mighty touchy around here about crowds."

"Jacques wasn't doing anything," Ben mumbled.

Luther sighed. "Don't fret yourself about it, boy," he advised. "The only thing that could maybe help them would be money. Likely they'll be turned loose tomorrow anyhow."

As soon as he was through eating, Ben despondently clumped up the rickety stairs to his room. It was hotter up there under the eaves. He looked across the rooftops and thought how complicated things were in a big town.

Restlessly he trotted back downstairs and on out to the cowshed, where the oxen were chewing contentedly. The smoke from Luther's pipe drifted around from the front steps, for it had grown a little breezy. Ben leaned heavily against the corner pole of the shed. The sad-looking cow and the packhorse were gone; Luther had apparently sold them.

He was startled when Libby's breathless voice spoke his name. She had come like a wraith on her bare feet and now stood close to him.

"It came to my mind that I could do something," she said hesitantly. Her loose hair nearly covered her eyes, but Ben caught a glimpse of a small crooked smile.

"Do what?"

"I know where the jail is," she said with bitterness in her soft voice. "They took my father there for debts once. That's why I was bound out."

"Listen," Ben said quickly, "take me there."

"Uh-uh," she said, shaking her head. "T'wouldn't do. But I could bear a message. The watch knows me, and if I had to, I could say I've come for the doctor 'cause Mrs. Greene's took bad."

There was a note of amusement in her voice, and her one dimple flashed. Ben could see the humor in trying to imagine the invincible Mother Greene ailing; he had a feeling she could glare a fever right out of the house.

"Well—here, then." Ben dug out his coins. He needed another shilling to finish paying for his breeches and at least four for the shoes. Beyond that he had two shillings and the Spanish money. Ben wrinkled his forehead and wished passionately that he could remember more about money. He pressed the two shillings into Libby's hand.

"Take these," he commanded. "And here . . ." He felt in

his pockets and pulled out a coil of rawhide. "Take this, too."

Then his fingers brushed the banana, now growing soft. "Oh, wait. Would you like this?"

Libby's eyes glinted behind the tangle of hair. "My stars," she whispered, "I've never had one."

"Be sure you peel it," Ben said grandly.

"I mustn't dawdle," Libby breathed. "Thank you. I'll bring you word." She slipped away, and Ben walked around to join Luther on the front steps. He felt a little better.

Luther removed his pipe and scratched his beard. "You never did tell me how you made out with your buying. Spread your money from one end of Back Street to the other, like a sailor who's not seen shore for six months?"

"Not so's you'd notice," Ben objected. "Bought me some shoes, and you saw the broom I got for Ma."

"You might have got mixed into more than you bargained for," Luther said severely. "I never had trouble with the authorities in this town, and I don't look to now. Appears to me you're too apt to jump and then study on it later. Mark you, walk the straight and narrow path around here, or you're not likely to walk this way again."

Luther went back to his pipe. Ben considered the situation in silence. Did Luther's remark mean that he had a chance of making another trip? Perhaps he hadn't been doing as well as he should, but look at all the experience he was getting. Ben resolved to be a model of moderation for the remainder of the trip.

A little later, as he settled down on the rustling cornshuck mattress, his thoughts turned again to Jacques. He had heard nothing from Libby. Why had he let a slight girl like her go off in the dark on such an errand? What if she ran into a bunch of toughs? Suppose the jailer caught her slipping something to Jacques? The cornshucks rustled louder as Ben tossed and turned. It was very late before he got to sleep.

The sky was gray the next morning, and the wind was gusty. Luther went off with a curt order to Ben to bide where he was for a while. Ben was glad because he had not had an opportunity to talk to Libby. He had been tremendously relieved to see her moving quietly about the fireplace as usual when he came downstairs.

"Drat the weather," Mother Greene sputtered, her hands planted on her hips and her frown challenging the clouds. "Rain or no rain, I've planned to do the washing, and wash I will, for the starch is made. Libby, don't just stand there. Fetch the bucket."

Libby vanished into the yard and Ben followed. "What happened?" he asked quickly.

Libby was filling the big washtub and she didn't pause. "I saw him," she said without looking around.

"Did you give him the money?"

"The jail keeper gave me a fit," she said, her flat little voice hardly above a whisper. "I told him I was Jacques' sister and had to see him." Libby turned tragic eyes on Ben. "I had to bribe him with my banana before he'd let Jacques come to the door."

"I'll get you another one," Ben promised recklessly. "How was Jacques?"

"All right. He's a clever one. The jailer must have told him his sister was there to see him because he put his arm around me and said, 'How is Ma?' " Libby smiled lopsidedly and there was a touch of color in her pale cheeks. "The wind was making the candle flicker, and it was no trouble to pass him the things you sent."

"Did he say anything?"

"Well, he couldn't much, because of the jail keeper, you know. But you could tell he was glad."

"That's a load off my mind." Ben sighed. "Now if he just gets out all right . . ."

"Lib-e-e-e!" called Mother Greene impatiently. "Where *is* that girl? Libby, I declare, you get slower by the minute. That tub isn't half full yet."

"Let me," said Ben hastily, making a grab for the bucket.

"I'll get the pail of soap," Libby said breathlessly, and fled toward the kitchen.

Ben was emptying the last bucket of water when Luther came into the yard. He hoped Luther hadn't noticed the kind of work he was doing. "The *Roxie A.* is standing on and off outside until the weather will let her in," the trader told him. "May be three or four hours before she can tie up."

"That gives me time to pick up my shoes and breeches," Ben said.

"Time first to give the steers a good currying," Luther said casually, "and grease the axles. We'll be heading for home before long. Might be a wheel spoke that could stand tightening, too."

Ben took off his jacket. Looked as though Luther figured to keep him too busy to get into trouble. While he worked, Luther checked through his load, lashing down barrels and stowing bundles snugly. Libby trotted busily between the house and the fire where water was heating in a big black kettle. Mother Greene appeared once, deftly chopped a couple of lengths of wood to her taste, and shoved the pieces under the kettle.

When team and load finally were shipshape, Luther said Ben had better get on with his business. Ben needed no urging, but before he left, he put a pair of clean stockings in his pocket.

On the street, he hesitated, realizing for the first time that he wasn't quite sure of the way to the cobbler's shop. That was a mighty roundabout way he and Jacques had gone. It was hard to keep your direction when the lay of the land was all cluttered up with buildings. Ben turned back to get Libby's help again.

Libby straightened up from the scrubbing board and brushed back her hair with a wet wrist.

"What I need is some landmarks," Ben said ruefully.

Libby smiled. She figured out some simple directions and gave them to him. "Mind now—turn at the sign of the anchor," she said in her thin voice.

Ben was elated when he found himself in front of the cobbler's shop. Who said he didn't know his way around town?

"Good morning," the elderly cobbler greeted him cheerfully. "Here you are, young sir, and let's see to the fit."

Ben sat down and pulled out his rolled-up stockings. As he did, he felt another lump in the depths of his pocket. It was Jacques' cap. He should have sent it back with Libby last night.

The shoes felt heavy and stiff to Ben, and he stepped about the shop for a moment to get the feel of them. One thing about moccasins—they didn't bind your feet.

"Seem to fit fine," remarked the cobbler.

Ben guessed he'd get used to them in time. He brought out his last crown and was given a shilling in change. He was relieved, for if the boots had cost any more, he'd have been in trouble.

"I'd thought to take the old ones with me, too," he said uncomfortably as he regarded his worn moccasins.

"To be sure," agreed the cobbler, as he found a torn piece of sacking and wrapped up the old shoes.

Ben clumped off in high spirits toward the tailor shop, retracing the route he and Jacques had taken. Somewhere he missed a turn, and finally had to ask directions to Grimes' store. By the time he saw the familiar door, he was disgusted with himself for getting lost and irritated because his feet hurt.

XV

Counterfeit!

◆————◖◗————◆

Ben entered the tailor shop and stood waiting. One of the tailors glanced up briefly and bent again over his needle. Ben cleared his throat loudly, and at that the stooped clerk appeared in the opposite doorway.

"Oh, it's you," he said disagreeably. In his thin fingers, he held a pair of scissors with wicked points.

"Are they ready?"

The clerk smiled in a nasty way and looked at a point over Ben's head. "I'm afraid not," he said. "Mr. Grimes did not feel that, under the circumstances, the alterations should be made."

"Why not?" Ben demanded.

The clerk waved the scissors negligently. "I didn't recommend that the transaction be completed," he said. He walked to a table and touched the folded breeches lying there. "Really, we couldn't let something like this go . . ." he looked Ben up and down meaningfully. "Mr. Grimes bade me give you this—your advance payment." He reached into a drawer, stepped delicately across the room, and put a shilling and a piece of paper into Ben's hands.

Ben looked blankly at the paper. *"That's* not my money," he choked.

"My dear fellow," the clerk said impatiently, "don't you know United States currency when you see it? Oh, of course— you probably can't read. Well, that's a new one-dollar bill. It's the equal of four shillings."

He opened the door and pushed Ben's shoulder, and Ben found himself standing in the street shaking with rage. Of all the low-down, conniving . . . He glared at the paper in his hand. Of course he could see what it said: *The Bank of North America*. It was just like the one that the schoolmaster had been using as a bookmark. There was the design and there the amount. The amount was the only difference, for Mr. Hammond's note had been for five dollars. There was the little extra line in the corner that he had said was a flaw . . . Ben squinted in horrified disbelief. There were the little nicks where the engraver hadn't been quite equal to the involved design!

"It's counterfeit!" Ben said aloud, hoarsely. Those dirty thieves! They wouldn't give him his breeches, and now they had stolen his good money.

Ben whirled on his heel and slammed back into the shop. "You'll not put it over on me!" he shouted to the startled tailor, as he strode across the room and grabbed up the blue breeches. The clerk twisted his long neck around the door frame. "What is the meaning of this?" he bleated.

"Mark you!" Ben said wildly. "You've tried to swindle the wrong man. Tell your fancy employer that!"

His eyes glittering, the clerk came through the doorway with a rush, raising the slender shears like a stiletto. Ben ran for the open door, half-turned as he dove through, and instinctively flung up the hand that held the bundled moccasins. He felt a sharp, stinging blow. Then he was free of the building and running like a scared rabbit down the street.

A high discord of shouts followed him. People on the street

jumped anxiously to one side as he plunged by, and a little girl ran shrieking to her mother. A glance over his shoulder showed him that at least three men were in pursuit. The clerk led them, lifting his knees high as he ran and yelling his lungs out.

Ben wished he had on his moccasins. He streaked past the corner where Jacques had come to grief the night before and bolted up the street toward Mother Greene's. Where could he hide? He looked desperately right and left, but saw no place where he could turn. Finally, he plunged down the alley between Mother Greene's and the tall house next door just as his panting followers turned the corner.

"There he goes!" shouted the clerk. "We've got him."

Ben's long legs skimmed over the high board fence, and he fell like a rag doll into the onion bed, dropping his new breeches and his bundle. He staggered over to the wagon and there, disheveled and panting, he stood at bay.

Mother Greene whirled from the clothesline where she was hanging sheets, and Libby dropped the garment she was wringing.

"Who's at odds?" Mother Greene asked forbiddingly.

"They tried to keep my new breeches and my money, too," Ben gasped, almost weeping with frustration.

A babble of voices swelled and receded beyond the fence as the searchers combed the yard next door.

"We'll have to call the sheriff!" someone shouted.

"What! Let that robber get a mile away?" asked another. "I tell you he's here somewhere, and I'll make it my business to keep him until the sheriff is brought."

Mother Green lifted a long, dark skirt from the pile of soiled laundry waiting beside the tub. "Pull it on," she muttered fiercely. "Hurry, you dolt, step in!"

Like a sleepwalker, Ben struggled into the skirt. Mother Greene whipped a shawl over his head and knotted it under his chin. She yanked it forward over his eyes.

"All right, scrub!" she commanded, with a shove toward the tub. "Libby, quick! Get the things Ben dropped in the onion bed and go inside and hide."

Libby vanished. Ben pulled something out of the gray, soapy water and rubbed it awkwardly on the slatted board.

Like a pack of hounds, the searchers rounded the corner of the house. Mother Greene stepped in front of the sheet she had just hung up and stopped them with a glance. "What's all this?"

A jumble of explanations shot at her. "Threatened this man, here." "Where is he?"

Mother Greene's eyes shot sparks. "Is this all you can find to do—upsetting an old woman at her work? You can see for yourself there's nobody here but me and my bound girl."

The men looked helplessly about. It was true that the yard was too small to hide much of anything. Behind the flapping sheet, Ben bowed over the tub and scrubbed for dear life.

"Well, he could have run into the house," cried the clerk. "We want a look, we do!"

"Look away," invited Mother Greene ominously, "but heaven help the man who muddies my clean kitchen floor."

The clerk leaped up the steps and lifted the latch of the kitchen door. Apparently he was fast losing his enthusiasm for investigation, because he only peered into the room and shut the door again.

"Are you satisfied?" shrilled Mother Greene, her elbows jutting dangerously. "Now be off—the whole worthless pack of you!"

The men moved back toward the street, arguing among themselves. When they were all gone, Mother Greene stalked over and tugged the shawl from Ben's head. "You'll do well to stop scrubbing that waist," she told him sharply, "before you've rubbed it clean through."

Ben stumbled over and collapsed on the wagon tongue. Soapy water dripped from his limp hands.

Mother Greene eyed his sagging face and laughed. "Count yourself lucky that you've not grown a beard yet." She chuckled. "I saw one of those ninnies inspecting you pretty sharp."

Libby appeared from somewhere. In her arms, she carried the disputed breeches and Ben's bundle. Sticking clear through the bundle were the clerk's long scissors. Suddenly Ben realized that the soap was stinging his hands and he found a small puncture where the scissors had stabbed one of his palms. Well, another hole in the old moccasins wouldn't make much difference, and they had saved his hand from bad injury.

"That's a mighty fine pair of shears," Mother Greene remarked, drawing them from the package.

"Would you like them?" Ben asked humbly. "Take them and welcome. But would you—you wouldn't need to say anything about them to Luther, would you?"

"Or about the ruckus?" Mother Greene's sharp black eyes bored into Ben's.

"No, ma'am. I mean, yes, ma'am. I'd be obliged if you didn't. Luther's got some idea that I'm a little hasty," Ben confessed.

Mother Greene sniffed. "Well, seems like it'd be poor business to lose the shears," she said. "For pity's sake, Libby, are you going to stand around gawking all morning?"

Ben was left to arrange himself as best he could and wait for Luther. He took off the shoes and stockings and slipped on his old moccasins. He thought he'd wait until they got out of Portland before he tried the stiff shoes again. You never knew when you'd have to run for it in this worrisome place.

When Luther came, he was preoccupied with getting the wagon under way and seemed to notice nothing strange in Ben's silence. Ben wished they might stay for dinner, but nobody mentioned it.

As the oxen stood ready to pull out, he hurried to the

corner of the yard where Libby worked. "I've got to go," he said uncomfortably. "I'm sorry I didn't get you another banana." He pulled a butter stamp out of the big game pocket of his hunting jacket and offered it to her. "Would you like this? Maybe you could sell it. I carved it myself."

The stamp showed a crude fir tree cut into the center and crosshatches forming diamonds spreading out to the corners. Libby held the wooden handle tightly. "I'll try to get word of your friend," she said shyly.

"When I come back again," he said. He trotted away without saying good-by. He hoped she'd have word for him—*if* he came back again.

The confusion on Fore Street hadn't changed much since yesterday, but the sunshine had given way to low clouds and a blustery wind. Vessels moved restlessly at their moorings. The heaving waters of Casco Bay looked cold and gray under the fog bank.

The *Roxie A.* creaked complainingly as the waves, chasing each other endlessly landward, crashed against her streaming sides. Luther sought out Captain Dow, who was checking his manifest as the kegs and barrels trundled by him. Ben edged closer to the plank and finally made his way up to the hatchway from which the trade goods were being lifted.

He was filled with delight. His feet were on the deck of a ship—a real seagoing ship that had seen the shores of India and the Spice Islands. He turned to watch a barefooted young deck hand who was making motions with some sort of a cleaning tool but not seeming to accomplish much. Then the blond sailor left off working entirely and stared at Ben.

"What kind of ship is this?" Ben finally ventured to ask.

"Just a rotten old schooner," the blond boy said indifferently. "Never see a schooner before?"

"Well," Ben said defensively, "you don't see many boats

where there's no more'n three feet of water." He decided to change the subject. "What's up there?" he asked.

The barefooted lad turned. "That's the forecastle," he said. "Aft's the deckhouse. The cabin's below. Not much bigger'n a hencoop. Galley's on the port side. The whole midships is cargo space."

Ben looked up at the masts and the web of lines.

"We ran into some weather yesterday," the boy commented. "Took some seas aboard. Didn't dare to sheet the mains'l home and were mortal slow getting here."

Ben was wide-eyed with interest although he didn't understand much of the talk.

"You're from the mountains?" the sailor asked.

"Uh-huh."

"Listen, mate," the boy said eagerly. "How do you hold off the Injuns when you're hauling through the mountain passes? Won't the bloody savages knife you in your sleep?"

"Aw, no!" Ben exclaimed. He could hardly believe he wasn't being made sport of. "I've been through some of the roughest country between here and Canada and haven't yet seen a wild Indian."

"But they were waiting there, sneaking through the brush, ready to scalp you," insisted the sailor. "You wouldn't catch me afoot in those woods." He seemed full of admiration for Ben.

Ben put back his head and guffawed. "You'd be in more danger from skunks then you would from Indians!"

The blond boy's face turned red, and his eyes narrowed. Then his expression grew cunning.

"Cap'n Dow wants me below now," he said. "Suppose you keep an eye on the foremast for me. Got to make sure the—ah—boat's in trim. I'll be right back."

The top of the mast rocked back and forth as the deck heaved restlessly. When Ben kept his gaze on it, the horizon seemed to be doing the swinging rather than the mast. The white-flecked billows tumbled past, and the mist-veiled sky-line rose and fell. Ben began to feel uneasy.

He studied the weathered deck and the scarred railing. The young sailor didn't reappear. Ben shuffled his feet and eyed the mast. To his left, a row of larger craft heaved gently. Ben's stomach began to feel strange. He shook his head and swallowed. Where was that crazy lad?

Suddenly Ben knew that he wanted land under his feet. Plague take the silly mast. He staggered down the plank to the pier. Luther was winding up his business with Captain Dow.

"Did you decide to bear a hand, now that the work's done," he asked pointedly.

"Yes, sir," Ben gulped.

Luther studied Ben's pale face. "I be blowed!" he rasped. "You've gone and got yourself seasick, and the ship's in port!"

"No such thing," Ben said with dignity. He stumbled to the wagon and waited there, carefully keeping his eyes fixed on the street.

"There," said Luther, "I hope Amaziah wants this truck as bad as he let on."

Ben hunched his shoulders and followed the rumbling wagon away from the waterfront. The mist had closed in and seemed to mute the activities of the town.

Ben thought fleetingly that Mother Greene wasn't going to get her washing dry. He wished that he could sit down somewhere and ease his stomach, but he didn't want to waste any time getting out of town, either. The tailor's clerk might still be after him.

They camped that night in a grove of pines just outside Saccarrappa. Ben had hoped they would find a place under cover, for although the afternoon rain had stopped, he was pretty well wet through.

"Are there any roadhouses around here?" he had asked Luther.

Luther had said severely, "One night at Mother Greene's and you expect to be pampered like the governor's lady. Now get the critters unhitched."

Ben didn't really mind camping, for he was almost dry by the time they had eaten. As darkness fell, he leaned back against the rough bark of a giant pine and stared at the campfire. After a while, he became aware of a face beyond the wagon—two big eyes that showed in the flickering light. A branch on the fire crumbled and fell, sending a little shower of sparks into the night air. By the flare of light, Ben saw a child standing there.

"Well, come on over," he called. Luther shifted his weight on the wagon tongue so that he could see what was going on.

A small boy edged uncertainly toward the fire, dragging an even smaller child by the hand. Ben judged them to be brother and sister.

"How are you?" Luther asked politely.

"Bien," mumbled the boy faintly.

"Have a seat," Ben invited the youngsters, pointing to a folded cowhide that lay near the fire. The two sat down, crossed their legs Indian fashion, and regarded Ben solemnly.

"Any of that johnnycake left?" Luther asked.

"Naw," Ben admitted, feeling guilty. "I finished it."

The four of them studied each other in companionable silence. Then the boy reached into his pocket and drew out a small gadget. When he put it to his lips and began to hum, Ben realized it was a jew's-harp.

"Say, I'd like to get one of those for Goody," Ben said after the boy finished. "Hope we see a peddler on the way tomorrow."

"If you're so set on having one, whyn't you dicker with Joe here? He could likely get another," Luther suggested, as he moved away to get something from the wagon.

When the child saw the money in Ben's hand, he smiled with quick understanding. He leaped to his feet and brought the jew's-harp to Ben. Ben tried a tune, but the gadget only amplified the doleful sound of his voice. "Seems to work fine," he said with an embarrassed look. "Will you be able to get another one, Joe?"

Joe's eyes flashed. Maybe his name really was Joe. "It is nothing," he said with a dramatic wave of his hand. "I watch the road. I see the peddlers coming. I see everything!"

"Do you watch the timber trucks, too?"

"But, yes, of course."

"You wouldn't know Alphonse Dufresne?" Ben asked hopefully.

Not know Alphonse Dufresne! Joe was disgusted. Like his own father he knew M'sieur Dufresne. Why, he and Jacques had passed by this very day!

"You're sure?" Ben asked, his face lighting up. Joe's feelings were hurt. He did not wish to be taken for a person of no intelligence. Plainly he had seen them.

Ben felt like shouting for joy. Jacques had gotten out of jail. He was free! If Luther let him keep traveling, Ben felt positive he would see Jacques again. He dug in his pocket and pulled out the blue stocking cap. "Here," he said to little Joe, "give this to Jacques next time they pass by here. Tell him that Ben Tanner found it and that Ben hopes to see him again someday." He smoothed the lad's ruffled hair and persuaded him to give them another tune on the jew's-harp that was now Goody's present.

Presently a high-pitched shout called the children away.

Luther returned to the fire to knock out his pipe. "Just before we left," he mused, "there was a ruckus of some sort right near Mother Greene's. Heard tell the sheriff's men were looking for some young fellow who tore up a tailor shop."

Ben drew in his breath to make an indignant denial, but caught himself in time. "I heard some yelling," he said carefully.

"That's the trouble with most young rascals," Luther said severely. "No respect for law and order. And *you* attract trouble like a jug of molasses draws flies. Don't let me catch you getting mixed up in anything dishonest."

Ben's eyes were bleak as he stared at the fire. What law and order was he supposed to respect? Law that would jail a man for applauding another who spoke out for justice? Order of a kind that let counterfeiters operate on a large scale?

"One thing about Plin," Luther observed, "he can smell trouble coming and keep out of the way."

In the darkness Ben clenched his fists and glared. You bet Plin would keep away from anything rough!

XVI

Homeward Bound

———— ⸙⸎⸙ ————

Sunrise was only a streak of pink at their backs when Ben and Luther headed northwest toward Sebago Lake. At around noontime, they met a notions peddler with a fine big pack.

Luther stopped a moment and hailed him. "Little tad just this side of Saccarrappa waiting to do business with you," he said. "Keep an eye out, friend."

"Always got an eye for business," the young fellow said cheerfully. "Much obliged."

Luther kept them traveling long after dusk that evening. They were almost at the river crossing before the oxen were unyoked and turned out to feed.

Ben was more nervous about fording the Saco than he cared to admit, although Luther estimated that the wagon was lighter by several hundred pounds than it had been going east. Ben remembered all too well his experience in crossing the Connecticut.

His state of mind wasn't helped any when they arrived at the fast-running river and came upon an ox driver who was so angry that his face was purple. He had just completed the crossing, and the evidence of his disaster was floating rapidly away on the rushing water. Apparently the lumber that he had been hauling, lashed to two heavy trucks, had shifted and broken away and was now on its way to the coast without him.

"This is the last time!" he yelled. "I'm turning these— these goats out right here. I'm boarding the next raft that comes by and never setting my feet on land again!"

"Do tell," Luther said in a conversational tone.

"By mighty, I do!" The angry driver stalked over to his team.

"You actually going to turn the cattle loose and leave 'em?" Luther asked. He stepped to the side of the nigh ox and ran his hand down its wet foreleg.

"Watch me."

"Well, now, you don't want to be hasty," Luther admonished. He took a quick look at the teeth of the other black and white steer and straightened up suddenly. "Reckon they're not your oxen then," he stated.

"Who says that? Didn't I trade my skiff and my nets for the blasted critters? More fool, I! But I've learned my lesson and I'm going back to Casco Bay."

Luther planted his feet wide apart, rocked back on his heels, and hooked his thumbs in his belt. "Mark you, friend," he said, peering keenly at the upset teamster, "I'm not arguing your point—but I don't like to see waste, and that's what it would be if you turned those steers out here. Thin they are, but I judge them sound. No telling who'll pick them up. Now, why don't we try to fix up a trade that'll set well with both of us?"

Ben dangled his legs from the tailgate and watched as his stocky employer completed the swap for the span of oxen. A paper was drawn up and signed. "Just so we'll have proof of the way of it," Luther commented. "Sometime when the fish quit biting you might forget you sold 'em."

"In a pig's eye!" snarled the teamster.

As part of the bargain, he was fitted out with a bag of provisions from such as the wagon carried. He shouldered the bag and went striding off eastward without another look.

"Hey, what do you call the steers?" Luther yelled after him. "Or does it bear repeating?"

"Cap'n and Mate," came the faint reply.

Luther walked around his new team. "Well, boys, I hate to make you head back across the river, but it's a long way around it," he said with a cheerful ring in his voice.

Ben dreaded the idea of taking the first step into the rolling river. He felt even worse when he saw the wall-eyed stare that the new lead oxen wore as their sharp hoofs slipped and skidded down the pebbly bank. The last crossing was still fresh in their minds.

Luther shuffled alongside, his goad clenched in his fist and with a grim look on his bearded face. Water dashed against the bellies of the oxen, then crept high on their sides as they worked toward midstream. The cold water tugged at Ben's legs.

Suddenly, the off ox slipped and half-fell against the nigh animal, staggering him, but Luther was quick to grab the massive horns until both were standing firmly again. Dripping white at the muzzle, the new steers nervously moved forward again, followed with calm deliberation by the wheel span. Buck and Star were not ones to be easily shaken. Where Luther led, they followed, though the weight of the wagon bowed their heavy necks to the surface of the water.

To Ben's immense relief, the wagon soon rose with a great gurgling and splashing of the high wheels until it was in water not much more than knee-deep. By quartering across the stream, they stayed with the gravel bar until they were nearly to the other bank. Then a few feet of deep water had to be crossed, and at one point Star had to swim a little, but the bank was close and the oxen eager to reach it.

In a few moments, the wagon rocked triumphantly up the

slight grade, and the oxen stood blowing while Luther and Ben checked the load. Luther was well pleased with the performance of his new span.

"That feller must just be handier with an oar than a goad," he observed.

With the help of the extra team of oxen, Ben and Luther made good time on the homeward trail. They crossed the New Hampshire line and wound their way through the intervales, enjoying clear weather. The peaks of the White Hills rose ever nearer and darker against the summer sky, and the road grew lonesome.

They camped below the lower opening of the notch. Ben sprawled beside the fire and listened to the rush of the Saco River. Tomorrow would see the worst of the journey over— if they were lucky. Ben knew he would be glad to get back. He was thinking of pie—cold milk and fresh-baked pie.

"Next trip, maybe I'll just bring along a pack animal," Luther said, half to himself. "I'll drive as big a herd of cattle as I can pick up—while the grass is good. When the feed's poor, they shrink too much."

Ben forgot about pie. Suddenly worried, he waited for Luther to go on, but the burly wagoner only chewed on his pipe stem. Surely Luther would want his help with a whole herd to shove along and with skittish yearlings that would be constantly ducking into the softwoods.

"I'm a fast runner," Ben observed. "You'll need me to keep the stragglers out of the brush."

Luther's heavy brows drew together. He scratched his whiskers and stuck out his lower lip. "That remains to be seen," he said finally.

Ben didn't call that a very satisfactory answer. He went to sleep worrying.

Coming down through the notch had been a task; going

back was a real battle for men and animals. Ben shoved until his eyes blurred. He rolled big rocks to one side and
dropped small ones in potholes. He stumbled along beside
the lead team, flicking a birch switch at their straining flanks.
The stiff branches of fallen spruce scratched a stinging net-
work on his face and arms as the trail twisted up the great
gully.

They crawled upward along a spine of bare rock that
sloped steeply down to the river. The oxen moved ahead
cautiously, hesitated as a wheel caught, and came to a halt.

"Hup!" Luther yelled. "Ho there, Star!"

Buck and Star set their shoulders and pulled, but the lead
span lunged nervously, settled back, and then lunged again.
The newly acquired steers were bewildered and they side-
stepped uncertainly. Slowly the weighted wagon began to roll
backward. Luther jumped to drop the block chain, slipped
on the moss, and fell heavily on his side.

Ben was trying to calm the lead team as he saw Luther
fall. He stared with horror as the man lay still. The wagon
continued to roll backward, dragging the oxen with it, so
Ben dropped his switch and clattered back toward the load.
The oxen scrambled for footing as the wagon rolled faster.
Ben was afraid the angle of the hill was so steep that the
wagon would skid backward even if he could rig the block
in time.

Desperately he searched for a loose stone. With the whole
country made of rocks, why couldn't he find—ah! With a
blind rush, Ben tore up a half-buried rock and ran for the
nearest wheel of the wagon. His feet seemed to drag as the
wagon moved faster, and the steers snorted in fright.

Ben flung himself at the wagon, jammed the stone behind
the wheel, and prayed that it would hold. The wagon came
to a grinding stop, and he gave a thankful sigh. He tried to
speak reassuringly to the oxen, but he was too breathless.

Luther heaved himself to a sitting position and shook his

head groggily. His battered hat had rolled away, and Ben saw the beginning of a purple lump above one eye. He rescued the hat and dropped to his heels before Luther.

"You hurt bad?" he asked anxiously.

"Don't feel very good and that's a fact," Luther answered. "Give me a hand up." He felt his head gently. "Never had a better goose egg than that," he muttered. "The wagon all right?"

"For now. I trigged the wheel."

Luther wobbled forward and picked up his fallen goad. "Follow behind with your stone then, and let's get shut of this place," he rasped.

A few minutes later, the wagon rumbled safely over the top of the grade and stopped on level ground. Luther rapped the neck of the off ox, waved the other forward, and they turned smartly to the right and drew up under the leaves of a yellow birch.

"Turn 'em out, Ben," Luther said and dropped heavily to a seat on a mica-flecked granite boulder.

Ben was glad to busy himself with the unyoking. His legs were still trembling with tiredness and fright.

Later, as they sat wearily by the fire, Ben asked Luther whether it wouldn't be worthwhile, with so many northern Vermont towns beginning to have trade with Portland, to hire someone to fix up the trail a little.

"Fact is," Luther answered, "there's talk of making a turnpike all way to the Connecticut River. Be a fine road—one a grandmother could drive a carriage on without cracking the eggs in her basket."

"Oh, certain sure!" Ben said with vast disbelief. "And someday we'll load our goods on a wagon with wings and *fly* 'em to Portland."

Because of the early stop after Luther's fall, Ben and the trader were unable to make Littleton the next day. They

pulled into Alphy's tavern yard just before noon on the day
following and were greeted warmly by Fanny. Alphy was
swinging his scythe in the hayfield behind the tavern. He
left his mowing and hurried to meet them.

"Hope you brought the cinnamon," he called. "Otherwise,
Fanny's apt to run me off the place, and you, too."

"Got it," Luther assured him.

Fanny dished up dinner in a great flurry of spoons and
gossip, and the men fell to with appreciation. Afterward,
they sat in the shade of the maple beside the cowshed.

"How did you like Portland?" Alphy asked Ben.

"Say, that's quite a place!" Ben replied with enthusiasm.

"Seems busier every time I go there," Luther commented
as he tamped tobacco into his pipe. "Even during the slow
months on the West Indies run, there's enough coastal trade
to keep the pier humming. Looks to be more business inland,
too."

"S'truth," agreed Alphy. "Business *is* good. Been a deal of
traveling men on the road."

"I recall there was one here the night we came through
heading south," Luther said.

"Ayah. Mighty fancy, he was. Say, do you recollect the
oldster who was here the same evening? Skinny old man with
a scar? Well, next I heard of him, the constable up to Danville picked him up for spreading counterfeit money. Had
some on him."

"Do tell!" Luther was mildly astonished. "Wasn't he a
pensioner?"

"He was. Collecting his veteran's pension regular. They've
got him confined to the jail limits."

"Well, the limits at Danville are near the size of a farm, so
they'll keep him busy setting rabbit snares or planting peas
till the next time the judge comes round." Luther chuckled.

"I hear the old pensioner is spending his time writing letters of protest," Alphy said. "Blames everything on the gov-

ernment. Says an honest man can't get along under President Adams, and claims he never saw the bad money before."

Luther shook his head. "And it right in his own pocket!"

"To me, the odd thing about it is how the constable came to catch him. Constable's mighty busy with his haying right now and not given to stopping travelers to see what kind of money they're carrying."

"Chances are good that he could stop every third man on the road and uncover money that wasn't right—if the fellow had any at all," Luther remarked. "A body does well to stick to barter these days."

Ben listened closely, for there was something strange about Alphy's tale. How did it happen that the old man landed in jail? If law officers went around poking in people's pockets . . . Ben thought of the counterfeit note in his own shirt. Suddenly it seemed as big as a newspaper.

Ben grew more and more impatient as the wagon rumbled slowly toward home. The rolling blue mass of the west fork of the Green Mountains looked familiar now. He was anxious to get across the Connecticut and feel Vermont under his feet again. He grinned to himself, remembering his impatience as they had approached Portland. Both ends of a trip seemed to be way ahead of the middle.

They crossed the state boundary as sunset streaked the ripples of the river with red. It seemed a pity to have to camp again so close to home, but Luther pulled off the road just beyond the scattered houses of Waterford. They watered the oxen at an obliging farmer's tub, sat awhile after supper on his doorstep, but declined the offer to bed down in his kitchen. It was pleasanter to roll up on the grass with the night song of summer insects to put them to sleep.

Tomorrow morning they'd pull into Amaziah's yard, and then there'd be a stir. Thinking of it, Ben fell asleep with a smile.

XVII

Bogus Banknote

By the time Ben and Luther reached East St. Johnsbury, there were many signs of activity. A small boy dawdled listlessly along the road until he noticed the trader coming. Ben was amused to see the sudden energy with which he made for the wagon. Luther handed out a couple of horehound candies and told him to bring his mother to Barber's store if he wanted any more.

They were hailed time and again as they neared St. Johnsbury Village. Ben felt as though he had been away a year. To make a grand impression at home, he had put on his new shoes and breeches right after they had crossed the Connecticut.

The sawmill was in full swing, and Ben could hear the whine of the saw long before they crossed the Passumpsic River bridge. Piles of fresh-cut boards stood under the trees on the river bank, and two dogs left off frolicking in the sawdust pile to yap a challenge to the oxen.

One of the sawyers, a shrunken little man whose clothes looked as though they were borrowed, spied the team and came from the shed.

"Well, Luther, ye made it back in jig time. Where'd ye get the new cattle?"

"Found 'em on the trail," Luther answered.

"Thought ye might have swapped Ben for 'em."

"Oh, I did try to turn him in on a barrel of salt, but the dealer wanted too much to boot."

"His hide wasn't prime, I expect," the sawyer said soberly. He turned suddenly and clapped Ben on the shoulder. "How'd ye like Portland, boy?"

"Fine, Dave," Ben said with a grin. "There's sure a lot of it."

"So I hear. Well, ye'll likely get better acquainted there— don't believe Luther will want that Plin along any more."

Ben's grin was wiped away, and his heart gave an unexpected thump.

"What makes you say that?" Luther asked.

"Why, the ungrateful scoundrel is dishonest. Amaziah caught him slipping bad money into the cash box. No telling how much he's cost the storekeeper. And after Letty taking care of him and all. 'Course, Letty's tongue is enough to put most any man on his feet in a hurry . . ." Dave snapped his knitted suspenders and laughed loudly.

Luther scowled. "That's an odd piece of business," he said. "Plin might not be much on work, but I'm bound I've never had a mite of trouble so far as money's concerned."

"Ha. Maybe ye just don't know what he's been about. He's tricky."

Luther looked grim. "How'd this all come to light?" he demanded.

"Plin got so's he could peg around some—Amaziah got somebody to shape a rough crutch for him—and he'd come out and sit by the counter and enter trade goods in the book and such as that. Mighty handy with his pen, and *fast*. Say, I watched him reckon up a line of figures about as long as my arm and he set down the sum quicker'n I can count my young 'uns. But that's the trouble with smart ones—you've got to watch 'em. Watch 'em good."

"I know how he ciphers," Luther said impatiently. "What about the money?"

"I'm telling ye!" Dave said. "While he was still in bed and evenings after he was up and around, Ben's brother would come down to the store and they'd read and Plin would show Will how to do sums. The schoolmaster came sometimes, too. Plin got so bold what with all the attention he was getting, that he'd even look ye straight in the eye. Letty found him a clean shirt and he—"

"Great galloping ghosts!" Luther slapped his leg in frustration. "I don't give a hoot about his shirt, you dunce. *What about the money?*"

Dave stared at him with a pained expression. "You sure are the most aggravating sort to try to tell anything to! Why don't ye stop gabbling and listen, then?"

Luther heaved a sigh and flung his arm over the wheel. Ben was in such a fever of anticipation that he couldn't stand still, but he was careful to keep quiet. One more interruption and Dave might go back into the mill, and then they wouldn't know the story till they'd got clear to Amaziah's store. And the storekeeper was apt to be close-mouthed, especially about his own affairs.

"Let's see now . . ." Dave rubbed his chin. "Ye went and made me lose the furrow with all your fuss. Anyway, a couple of days ago, Amaziah was going through the cash box—don't doubt but what he was thinking ahead to your wagon coming in—and there was this money. Well, he went straight to Plin, and Plin hemmed and hawed and allowed he didn't know a thing about it. He said there'd been only two customers with paper money that he knew of—Horace Cutler and a gentleman from Virginia who was traveling to Montreal. You know, he had the prettiest piece of horseflesh ever seen hereabouts. They say he was traveling in a gig, but he had to leave it down in the country somewhere after the roads got so bad. Now, why would a fellow like that, with his fancy gear and all, want to beat his way through the mountains just to get to Montreal?"

Dave lifted his shoulders and eyebrows in complete puzzlement. He looked to Luther for agreement, but the trader's black beard was quivering and his eyes had a dangerous glint.

"All right—all right!" the sawyer said hastily. "Plin thought about it a while, and then he remembered the southerner had had a note on the Bank of Massachusetts, and there it was, so that took care of him. So Amaziah lit out for Cutler's place so fast his coattail rattled."

Dave got to laughing and couldn't get his breath. Ben shifted from one foot to the other, wishing the talkative sawyer would get on with his tale. He had to grin, though, as he thought how Amaziah must have looked flying up the hill.

"What did Horace have to say to that?" Luther prompted.

"Horace hopped like a hen on a hot griddle." Dave tittered. "He stuck out his chest and waved his arms and called on heaven and the United States Congress to protect him from undeserved affronts by suspicious tradesmen.

"That didn't move Amaziah. He stuck to the issue and said the evidence pointed square at Horace. Horace got going again and told Amaziah he would overlook the unjust barbs of suspicion, and for Amaziah to remember who one of his best customers was and who could undoubtedly bring real business his way after he became active in the government of his new and vigorous state.

"Well, Amaziah said he wasn't voting just now and his store couldn't stay in a vigorous state with customers like Horace, and he'd better make good the money. Then Horace told Amaziah he wouldn't stand for any more accusations. He said he got the money he used for his buying from a well-to-do and very influential friend who had recently made a

business trip to see him—Horace's words, you understand,
not mine—and they had discussed politically important issues.
Then he allowed that if Amaziah had any sense, he'd look to
the serpent sheltered under his roof that was biting the hand
that fed it."

Dave hitched up his baggy breeches with his wrists and
paused to consider. "By mighty, *that* set Amaziah thinking,"
he continued, wagging his head judiciously. "He went
straight back to Plin and told him he aimed to get to the
bottom of the business if it took till snowfall. Plin got ugly
then and snapped and snarled like a cornered rat."

"It still won't add up," Luther muttered. "Where would
Plin get any money, good or bad? And if he had any, why
would he put it in Amaziah's cash box? Makes no sense."

"Agreed. But then, anybody with as miserable a disposition
as Plin's got probably did it for pure meanness of some sort.
Amaziah figured Plin got the counterfeit money somewhere,
took a good note out of the box, and slipped the bad one in
in its place. That way, he must have figured, he'd get rid of it,
and nobody the wiser."

"Did they find the good one?"

"Nope. They looked for it, though. That's when Plin got so
mad. I declare, if he'd been able to, he'd have killed somebody." Dave squinted at his audience. "And you know what?
Another bad note turned up in the book Plin was reading!"

"No!" exclaimed Ben.

"Yep. Well, that took the fight out of him. Never said
another word. Wouldn't talk to anybody and wouldn't give
any reasons for his evil actions. But I can tell ye, he looked
spiteful. Sort of shrunk up like a sour pickle."

"I wouldn't have thought it," Luther rasped.

Ben was torn between horror at Plin's thankless behavior
and joy that the irritating bound boy was no longer in the
way of his own hopes for continuing as Luther's traveling
companion. What could have possessed Plin to act so? Just

went to show that he'd been right about that little sneak. Couldn't even be decent to folks who were nice to him. Ben looked questioningly at Luther, but the trader was staring at the ground, a deep wrinkle of perplexity between his brows.

"What will ye do with him now?" Dave asked.

"Depends," Luther said shortly. He took up his goad and spoke to the drowsing oxen. With a rumble and squeak, the heavy wagon started on the last lap of its journey. Ben followed closely, his new shoes making deep imprints in the dusty road.

When they finally pulled into Barber's yard, Ben wasn't sure what to expect, but everything seemed quiet. Amaziah heard them and came down the back steps to meet them, his collar sagging away from his thin neck.

"Good day, 'Ziah," Luther said gravely. "Hear you had some trouble while I was away."

"Did have a mite," Amaziah admitted calmly. "Don't think there'll be any more, though. What say you come in for a taste of cider before you unload?"

"Don't mind if I do," Luther declared. He swept off his shapeless wreck of a hat and wiped his face on his sleeve.

Ben wasn't sure whether he'd been included in the invitation or not, but he tagged along anyway. He did not, however, get to hear the talk between Luther and Amaziah. They took their mugs and went on to the storeroom, leaving Ben to sit uneasily in the kitchen with Lettice, who only sniffed and went on kneading her bread dough. Plin wasn't anywhere in sight, and Ben didn't dare ask her anything about him. Presently, Letty was called into the front of the store by the arrival of customers, and he was left to twiddle his thumbs and wonder about Plin's odd behavior.

Before long, Luther returned and silently led the way out to the wagon. He and Ben wrestled the kegs and barrels into the storeroom and checked the tally sheet with Amaziah.

Luther handed the storekeeper a small bundle. "Tuck that someplace where it won't get smashed," he said. "Some sort of widget for the clockmaker up to Danville Green. The postboy will pick it up next time around."

"Ayah," Amaziah agreed.

Luther turned to Ben. "I'm taking Buck and Star on down to the blacksmith. You take the new team and the wagon along up to my place. Plin will ride with you. Stop at your house and let your ma know you're back if you've a mind to, but mind you don't let my barrel of molasses come to grief."

Ben looked sulky. That confounded molasses had got this far without mishap and it wasn't likely to come to harm in another four miles. He didn't relish the thought of Plin's company, either.

Ben unyoked the new team and hooked them up to replace Buck and Star on the pole. He started to break a branch from the lilac bush, thought with sudden guilt of his last run-in with Lettice, and decided it would be wiser to get his whip from a young maple over by the stone wall.

As Ben strode back to the wagon, stripping leaves from the slender switch as he walked, he saw Plin hitching his painful way down the steps. Plin's black hair drooped carelessly over his eyes, and his leg was splinted stiffly. Ben couldn't see any sign of improvement in his looks. When he grabbed Plin under the arms and boosted him into the wagon, Plin's eyes flashed a look of pure hatred. He crawled to a corner of the wagon and sank to the floor with his shoulders against the barrel of molasses. He laid his crutch and his bundle beside him and didn't look up again.

"Hysh, Cap'n," Ben cried cheerfully. He began to feel much better. As they wheeled ponderously into the Plain road, his chest swelled. He waved his whip with a flourish at Mrs. Johnson and another woman who were headed toward the store, skirts fluttering and tongues clacking.

"Why, it's Ben!" exclaimed Mrs. Johnson, peering at him. "Thought you were to Portland."

"I was, ma'am," Ben said, trying to sound matter-of-fact. "Just got back. Taking this new span home for Luther."

"Land sakes, I'm surprised to see you looking so hearty. Wasn't the trip dangerous? What about all those pirates and highwaymen?"

Ben tried to keep a sober face. "Oh, there's not much trouble with pirates in Portland," he assured her. "The roads are overrun with bad 'uns, though. Luther and I had a rough time with some of 'em, but we came out on top."

"My goodness, I'm glad I'm not your mother. I'd not be able to close my eyes at night while you were off being exposed to nobody knows what dangers and temptations. How she'll stand it if you go off again, I can't imagine. Likely the next trip Luther makes will be to Boston to shed himself of that miserable Plin." Mrs. Johnson grasped her shawl tightly and clucked her tongue. "You heard about Plin?"

"I heard," Ben said quickly. He didn't want Mrs. Johnson to get started on one of her endless lectures, although he took a wicked delight in knowing that Plin, hidden by the sideboards of the wagon, was forced to listen.

"It certainly is a caution," she said severely. "I deem it very lax of Amaziah not to take steps to protect honest folks from more trouble. The Danville stocks are the proper place for Plin, *I* say."

"Now, Serena, that's putting it pretty hard," objected her companion. "Will claims Plin didn't do it, and I don't believe Amaziah—"

"Will?" Ben asked with sudden interest.

"Yes, your brother," Mrs. Johnson answered. "When he heard, he ran straight for the store. He stuck up for Plin. Will's so quiet, you know, and never gets mixed up in anything like that. It was a real surprise to Amaziah. Will stood

there, all out of breath from running, with his face all dusty
and streaked with sweat, and *yelled* at the men who were
searching. He said they were a pack of wolves. Well, you can
imagine!"

"Did you see him?" Ben asked, not bothering to hide the
disbelief in his voice. He didn't think there was a word of
truth in her wild yarn. It must be an idea she'd picked up
from some other flighty female and then added her own fancy
stitches to it. Will wouldn't have gumption enough to open
his mouth.

"I certainly did. I was picking out some buttons when
Amaziah came back from Horace Cutler's. Poor man, he was
distracted. Then to have a half-grown squirt like that practically insult him—well! He told Will to take himself out of
there in a hurry. Will gave him an awful look and went off,
and I don't know but what he was crying. I must admit it
gave Amaziah a turn. He told one of the men from the mill
he thought maybe we all ought to let it go, and the problem
would likely work itself out, but right after that they found
more of the counterfeit money. Then there wasn't no doubt
in anybody's mind."

Ben felt hot with embarrassment. Why did Will want to
go and make the whole family look foolish? Ben could hardly
believe it, even now. The usually meek Will suddenly acting
like that . . .

"Got to be getting along," he mumbled quickly, tapped the
off ox, and got the wagon moving again before they could
involve him in the discussion. Pretty soon, he dropped back
so that he could look into the wagon. He was wondering
whether he dared ask Plin anything about the fuss. Plin,
sprawled on the floor, looked up contemptuously at Ben. "I
poison wells, too," he said with a curl of his lip.

Ben scowled and hustled back to the oxen. At least Plin
could have had the decency to be ashamed of himself.

As Ben headed up the hill, the barefooted Kent boys and

their small sister caught up with him. They were swinging birchbark pails filled with blueberries. They hailed him with excitement and danced along beside him.

"What did you bring back?"

"Did you see any ships, Ben?"

"What's it like beyond the White Hills?"

Then the tallest of them glanced over the tailgate and noticed Ben's surly passenger. Instantly there was a hush. The little girl's eyes grew wide with alarm; the boys nudged each other and whispered.

"Where you going, Ben?" asked one.

"I'm heading up to Luther Chickering's place," Ben said gruffly. He'd never seen the beat of the way this business had put the town on its ear. "How is it you're off picking berries when you're supposed to be in school?" he demanded.

"Aw, there's no school," the oldest boy said. "The schoolmaster's gone to Peacham. He went last week. I don't care if he never comes back."

"That's because you answered back, and he made you stay after school," his sister reminded him primly.

Ben felt sorry for the boys, cooped up like prisoners all through the summer days. "Well, go along now before you get run over," he said as he clumped steadily forward. He'd do well to reach Luther's house before supper.

Where the lane led to his own cabin, Ben stopped the steers. Chickens were scratching busily by the door, and he could smell freshly scythed hay. He craned his neck toward the crouching figure in the wagon. "I'll be back in two shakes," he told Plin.

"Don't see how I'll get along without you," Plin said with a sneer.

Goody came to the open door, wrinkled her forehead when she saw the unfamiliar team, and finally recognized Ben. She ran to meet him with a scream of delight. His mother hurried out to the step, a line of worry between her brows, and at the sight of her Ben's heart turned to melted butter. He was so happy to be home that he didn't know what to do next. He could only grin foolishly and hug his mother tight with one arm while Goody hung breathlessly to the other.

Then there was a wonderful bustle while Goody plied him with questions and Ma plied him with food. Ben felt like a prince.

"I can only stay a minute," he told them regretfully as he bit into a second blueberry muffin. "I've got to take the wagon on up to Luther's. But say—I brought you something, Ma. I'll go get it."

Goody scampered beside him to the wagon. Ben hoisted himself over the wheel and pulled out his pack. Then he handed over the broom. "Go give that to Ma and see what she says," he urged Goody with a wide grin. He felt in his pocket to be sure that he had her jew's-harp handy.

"Well, isn't that a wonder!" Ma was saying as he stepped across the sill again. She gaily whisked a piece of bark into the fireplace. Ben told her the tale of the new broom straw. Then he reached quickly into his hunting shirt and pulled out the jew's-harp. Goody's eyes grew round with wonder.

"What's it do?" she asked.

"It sort of sings," Ben said with a chuckle. "See, you hold it against your teeth like this . . ." He cleared his throat and self-consciously hummed a bar or two of *Yankee Doodle*.

"Oh!" squealed Goody. "Let me. Let me!" She popped the little instrument between her lips and twanged away with gusto.

"Benjamin, how good of you!" his mother exclaimed. "And you've got new breeches and shoes."

Ben regarded his feet with mixed feelings. He sure was proud of those shoes, but they seemed awfully cumbersome at times. "Luther says I'll never notice I've got 'em on, once they get broken in," he said with a doubtful note in his voice. "But say—these shoes have got to get on up the river right now. Tell Pa and Will I'm back, and I'll see you all to-morrow."

"I'll bake a custard pie," his mother called as he went out.

Ben walked on air. Everybody ought to take a trip, he thought. Made you see things in a different light. Made folks take a better look at *you,* too. Tomorrow he'd tell them all about Portland—or anyway, most of it.

XVIII

The Bear

❧ ———◦❀◦——— ❧

The sun was almost down when Ben turned west toward North Danville. He hadn't exchanged another word with Plin. The nearly empty wagon jolted along the shadowed road, with Luther's camp kit bundled next to the molasses barrel, and canvas covering and ropes piled beside it. An ax and a new pitchfork lay with Ben's rifle in the corner. The water keg swung beneath the wagon, and Ben stopped to get himself a drink. Silently he offered the dipper to Plin, thinking how glad he'd be to get rid of his scowling passenger and go back home.

A mile or so from Luther's place beside Sleeper's River, two boys hustled a bony cow across the road ahead of the wagon.

"Kind of late with the milking?" Ben inquired.

"Awful late," one of them admitted. "We couldn't find Brindle for awhile. She was down in the swamp and didn't want to come out. She keeps rolling her eyes and trying to hightail it back into the timber. I'm near done for, just getting her this far."

"Well, skedaddle, then, before she breaks away," Ben advised.

The boy hesitated. "You know what?" he asked finally. "I think there's a varmint down there that's got her skeered. I'm glad it's not dark yet." He took off with a rush as the cow bolted into the undergrowth.

Ben stood thoughtfully, flicking his switch in the dust. Nothing around here to bother a cow except a panther or a bear. Wolves always headed farther north in the summertime, and bobcats were too small to be anything more than a nuisance—except maybe to rabbits. Twilight would hold till nine o'clock or later, but in the swamp it would be dark and hard to investigate.

Plin poked his dark face up over the wagon box and knelt there, rubbing his backside. "You going to tear down into the brush and grab that bear by the ear?" he asked sarcastically.

Ben scowled. What he was planning was his own business, and he didn't like having his mind read. "Maybe I will and maybe I won't," he said.

"Why, this is your chance!" his tormentor insisted. "Likely he's been waiting for you to come back."

"Aw, keep quiet," Ben muttered. He still had some traveling to do before he got the steers home. Chances were mighty slim that he'd be able to find any kind of animal in that woods before night fell.

"Makes a difference when there's a real varmint around, doesn't it?" Plin jeered. "Or is it 'cause there's no brook to hide in?"

Ben whirled around with clenched fists. He stepped closer to the wagon. One more smart remark and Plin was going to be missing some teeth out of that provoking smile of his.

A sudden motion of the nigh ox took Ben's attention away from Plin. Cap'n had his head thrown back, and his nostrils were flaring. Mate shifted his feet nervously. Both steers were staring into the woods that sloped away south of the narrow road.

Whatever varmint it was, it must be close. Ben flung himself over the side of the wagon so that he could reach his gear. He swept up his gun, powderhorn, and bullet pouch and leaped back to the ground again. He loaded as swiftly as possible, his back turned to avoid Plin's mocking grin.

Then he moved quickly into the trees, regretting the heavy new shoes that made him feel clumsy. The rifle, though, hung smooth and balanced in his hand. His eyes flicked constantly through the openings in the swamp growth—under the branches of the gnarled black spruces, and behind the scattered boulders and bushes.

He was especially alert as he approached a half-dead swamp maple. If it was a panther that was bothering the stock . . . But no tawny body was stretched along the twisted limbs. Ben felt more and more certain that it was a bear that he was chasing, and that probably meant that he wasn't going to catch anything. Any self-respecting bear would be long gone into the depths of the swamp after the commotion made by the boys and his own rumbling wagon.

As he worked deeper into the woods, the ground grew spongy and rough. He bent down suddenly to examine a broad, fresh bear print in the mud. Water was still seeping into it. He straightened swiftly, and his mind had just time to observe how wrong his former thoughts had been when a big black brute started to come at him.

Ben raised his rifle, steadied, and fired within the space of a heartbeat, but his foot slid on the grass and the shot was only partly successful. The bear whirled with a heavy growl and bit at his flank. Ben took to his heels, fumbling with his bullet pouch as he ran. As he dodged through the trees, he marveled at the way of things. He'd bet a leg that it was the same ornery old bear.

Ben tried to reload his rifle as he ran at full speed. The footing was so bad . . . His fingers drew a twisted tube of paper from the bullet pouch. Pinching it carefully, he determined where the bullet lay, and bit off the opposite end. He cradled the rifle against his chest in an effort to hold it steady so that he could squeeze a pinch of powder into the priming pan. If he missed . . .

A steady crashing gallop behind him meant that he couldn't slow down. He was in sight of the road now—maybe the oxen and wagon would make the brute pause.

Ben dodged around a tree, doubled over for a minute, and managed to pour the rest of the powder down the gun barrel. Then he leaped forward again, poking the paper-wrapped ball into the muzzle. He prayed that his barrel wasn't fouled with black powder. Without a greased patch, the bullet might stick halfway down. He whirled at the edge of the road, well behind the wagon, and stumbled backward, frantically working with the gun and keeping an eye on the charging bear. One hind leg of the animal dragged, holding him back, but he came clumping on with savage determination, long teeth gleaming against the black cavern of his throat.

Ben pulled his ramrod loose with a frantic jerk. He wasn't going to be ready. Off a way to his right, he could hear the oxen blowing with fear. The yoke creaked, and something scraped over the floor of the wagon. Frightened out of their wits by the strong bear smell, the steers gave a convulsive leap and started to run. From the corner of his eye, Ben saw Plin standing at the tailgate, his arm raised. Then Plin was spun off balance by the yank of the team and toppled over the side of the wagon, but before he fell he had time to throw the pitchfork. With its sharp, curved tines shining, it flew straight at the bear's head.

This time there was a louder roar, and the bear staggered to a halt and clawed at his neck. Plin lay where he had fallen. With a sobbing breath, Ben raised the gun again and took careful aim. Black smoke filled his nose, but he saw the angry beast drop slackly as the bullet went true.

For a minute, Ben stood in the gray evening light holding

his gun in a limp hand. The coarse black pelt beside the road looked no more dangerous than a rug now. The rattle of the wagon had stopped, and everything was very quiet. Ben hurried to Plin, who lay face down in the dust, his rough crutch under him. Ben turned him over as gently as possible and tried to brush the dirt from his cheek. Ben bent and laid his ear to Plin's chest. At least he was alive.

He dragged the unconscious boy into the roadside weeds and put his crutch carefully beside him. Then he jogged up the road, wondering what had happened to the wagon and Luther's molasses. Suddenly Ben felt tired and discouraged. Luther was right to worry about leaving things in his care, he thought dully. He couldn't even be depended on to bring a practically empty wagon home. And no telling what was wrong with Plin. All because he couldn't let well enough alone, but had to go off in all directions—chasing bears or clerks or teamsters.

Ben pounded around a bend and came upon the team. The wagon was held fast by a big tree stump. Fortunately, the steers had apparently tried to turn the corner too sharply and had run a wheel against it. Ben checked the yoke and tongue, and looked at the barrel of molasses. To his dismay, he saw that there was a beaded brown line oozing along one of the staves.

With great effort, he managed to turn the team and drive back to Plin. He was relieved to see him sitting up, although his head was drooping. Ben urged the edgy steers back along the dim road until they stood trembling near the carcass of the bear. Then he unhitched the dipper and carried some water to Plin.

Plin's face was as white as his shirt, but everything else had gone gray and indistinct as night began to close in. When Ben dropped to his knees beside him, Plin raised his head. His eyes looked like holes burned in a blanket, but the fleeting smile he gave Ben was genuine.

"Jingo, when I came to and saw I was alone with that pile of bear over there, I nearly passed out again," he said hoarsely. "I didn't dare move an eyelash until I was sure he wasn't going to do any more damage. Good thing for me you know how to handle a gun."

"That bear did more damage than he was worth," Ben said wearily. "How are you feeling?"

"Gave my game leg a bad wrench," Plin answered. "Don't guess anything else is wrong."

Ben untied the tailgate of the wagon, lifted Plin carefully and put him down inside. He hied the oxen ahead, then dropped back and hoisted himself into the wagon beside Plin. He heaved a deep sigh as the wagon began to move. Then he turned to Plin. "Did you do it?" he asked, referring to the forged money.

"No!"

Ben went back to watching the road. If Plin wasn't responsible for the forged money, perhaps it had indeed been Cutler. Ben shook his head with dreary discouragement. Somewhere there must be an answer to this riddle, but he didn't see what he could do about it. One thing was sure; he was going to get rid of the forged note he was carrying. He felt for the stiff paper in his pocket. He'd like to show it to Will, but Will would be nosy about how he came by it. Ben didn't want to end up confined to the jail limits like that old farmer—the one who ran afoul of Grimes at the inn ... Ben's hands gripped the edge of the wagon body with sudden force, and he twisted to look at Plin again.

"Did Horace Cutler have a visitor a couple of weeks ago?" he asked. "Anybody see a potbellied dandy about town with him?"

Plin opened pain-filled eyes reluctantly. "*Everybody* saw him—Cutler made sure of that. He was a man from Portland and was supposed to be a bigwig in the Federalist setup. He bought some wool from Horace and promised to give him support when he runs for the Legislature."

"Did he go to Danville, too?"

Plin nodded. "Lyndonville and Peacham, too. Met with Amos Farley and Sam Goss—the two that put out the newspaper. He said the *Green Mountain Patriot* was a fine asset to the Federalist Party. Anyhow that's what Horace told everyone."

Ben's shoulders sagged further. It looked as though the whole story would have to come out—the money Grimes had slipped into the old farmer's breeches in the inn chamber, and the fight in Grimes' store. It was the little crackle of paper in his pocket that had brought Ben's thoughts into focus. The same little crackle he had heard the morning that he cowered under the quilt, hiding from Fanny. Ben's face grew warm as he thought how *that* little tale would sound, repeated at the forge and the mill. And Luther had made it all too plain how he felt about his associate's getting mixed up in violence and doing harm to the business.

Ben glanced with resentment at the dim form stretched out uncomfortably beside him. Plin might be hurt now, but he'd be back with Luther on the long haul to Boston. He'd be there, too, when the oxen lumbered into Montreal. And he, Ben, would be down in the potato patch, rapping his hoe on a rock and watching the geese fly over.

His thoughts were cut off as the oxen tried to turn toward the lights of a cabin that stood just in from the road. Ben dropped down and headed them off with a whack and a gloomy word. He knew just how they felt—they had had enough of traveling for one day and felt that their oats and hay were long overdue.

The road dipped, and Ben knew that Luther's place was just ahead. He trudged along dispiritedly beside the tired steers. This was the end of his journey. As they creaked into the yard, two of Luther's boys spied the team and came tumbling out of the door. Dogs began to bark, and excited shouts rang through the cabin. Betsy Chickering came quietly to the step with two little girls crowding close behind.

"It's just me, Mrs. Chickering," Ben called. "Luther'll be along any minute."

He pointed to the biggest boy. "You there—Arad, is it? Give me a hand with Plin?"

"He's with you?" Betsy Chickering asked, a shadow of worry crossing her placid brown face. "Let me help."

Between them, they got Plin up the steps and onto the settle before the fire. "I'll fix him up," said Luther's wife. "Girls, get back to bed."

"Where's Buck and Star?" asked one of the boys as Ben returned to the wagon.

"Coming," Ben said shortly. "Drive these critters into the barn and water 'em."

The boy turned the steers with a practiced hand, although his head barely came even with the tops of their shoulders. Ben got a rope from under the wagon and lashed it around the molasses barrel. He pulled the line as tight as he could. That would keep the sticky contents from leaking further, anyhow. As he knotted the rope, the boys dashed past the wagon and ran whooping down the road. Luther must be coming. Ben sat down on the chopping block and waited for him. Soon the trader drove his team into the barn and turned it over to the boys. He stopped beside Ben, took off his hat, and ran his blunt fingers through his hair.

"Best stretch of road in the world." He smiled. "Leads into my own yard. You wouldn't know anything about that bear I saw back a way? Fresh killed."

Ben nodded.

Luther's forehead wrinkled. "You're mighty glum about it. Isn't that just what you've been aiming at these many weeks?"

"Sprung your molasses barrel," Ben said morosely, "and that's not the half of it."

Luther's whiskers twitched as he hid a grin. "Well," he said gruffly, "Betsy and the babies are waiting. The rest can keep till morning."

Later, after a warmed-over supper, Ben lay on a pallet on the floor, sharing the covers with the boys, Samuel and Edmund. Plin had been given their bed. Ben squirmed a little and listened to the boys' soft breathing. Plin had gone right to sleep in spite of the pain in his leg. His actions had been surprising—the way he had balanced on one leg and thrown the pitchfork. Ben had been too busy at the time to think much about it, but it certainly wasn't the work of a coward, he realized now. Plin would no doubt even get to be a decent drover after a little more practice. Ben's throat began to ache, and it wasn't from lying on the hard floor. Letting go of a dream that had been his for so long was a hard thing to do.

Morning brought a flurry as the boys rushed to do their chores. Betsy fed the menfolk first, shooing the girls to the chimney corner to wait. Plin stayed in bed, and she sent Rhoda, blushing bashfully, to fetch him a mug of sweetened tea. Lumps of dark maple sugar were melting into the hot mush when Betsy brought it to the table, and the tea was fresh from Luther's pack.

"Hitch the new span of oxen to the cart," Luther told Arad, "and you can come along to help with that old bear Ben left back along the road."

Skinning the brute was quite a chore. He looked nearly as big in the daylight as he had the evening before, and his pelt showed scars of countless fights and one old bullet wound.

"He'll make a mighty nice, warm lap cover in the winter,"

Luther observed. "Unless your ma would rather have a rug."

Their knives moved rapidly. The boys lost interest after a while and wandered off to look for a fox den they thought was around there someplace.

"You know Plin about saved my neck last night," Ben said.

"That so?"

"He stopped the old devil with the pitchfork until I could get a shot into him. That's why he fell out of the wagon when the steers were spooked. Jolted the molasses barrel some."

"No great harm done."

"The other thing— Well, I'm sure it was Horace Cutler who passed that bad money—not Plin."

Luther straightened to ease his back and turned a stern eye on Ben. "You got a good reason to think so?"

"I believe Horace Cutler got the money the same place I got this," Ben said, pulling out the counterfeit note and passing it to Luther.

"Let's have the whole of it."

Ben started at the beginning. He slashed at the pelt as he talked; it made him less nervous to be doing something, and he didn't have to look at the trader.

"Probably Mr. Cutler just doesn't realize he's been hoodwinked," Ben wound up his painful account, "but I'm certain that's where the money came from. That other note—the one they found on Plin—likely it's the one the schoolmaster uses for a bookmark."

"That's a curious tale, if I ever heard one," Luther said darkly. "You think Grimes put the constable onto that old man when he was up in Danville?"

"That's my thought. I didn't see what Grimes was doing in the chamber, but I could hear pretty good. You know he got awful provoked the night before."

"Could be, could be," Luther muttered. "You been mighty quiet about all this till now. So it was you the Portland deputies were searching for, eh?"

Ben nodded without looking up.

In silence, they rolled the bear's pelt and heaved it onto the cart; then they hitched the unwilling oxen to the bear's carcass and dragged it down into the swamp. Luther whistled for the boys.

"Hurry back and tell your ma I've gone along to St. Johnsbury with Ben," he ordered.

XIX

Ben Tanner, Yankee Trader

When he and Luther approached the turn to his own cabin, Ben could hear the sound of a whetstone against a scythe blade. Pa must be mowing below the house. Luther pulled up in front of the barn.

"Throw off the hide," he said. "Better salt it as soon as you can. We'll go find your pa."

Ben smiled for the first time in hours as he caught sight of Pa and Will. Pa leaned on his scythe and listened with grave attention to the outline Luther gave him of the errand on which they were bent. Will looked pale and troubled.

When Luther mentioned the second forged note that had been found in Plin's book, Will exploded with angry words. "Those blundering numbskulls! I know where that note came from. Master Hammond lent me that book!"

"Ben told me," Luther said. "Now we've got to get on down and tell Amaziah."

Ben was enormously comforted when his father laid aside his scythe and straightened his straw hat. Pa was going with them. He was grateful, too, to Luther. His version of how Ben had come by the counterfeit note had been sketchy indeed, and there had been no mention at all of sheriff's deputies.

For the second time in two days Ben found himself in Letty's kitchen while the men talked outside.

"How's Plin?" she asked curtly as she came in from the store.

"Not so good," Ben mumbled, lost in his own thoughts. "Wrenched his leg when he threw the pitchfork at the bear."

"Are you daft?" Letty asked sharply. "Is that why your pa's talking with the others?"

Ben snapped out of his musing. "No, I'm not!" he said scornfully. "What they're talking about is Plin. And he did stick the bear with a pitchfork just before he fell out of the wagon last night. I've got the pelt up in the barn."

"My stars," Lettice said faintly. She looked completely flabbergasted and Ben felt a little better.

"Maybe they're thinking of setting the constable on Horace Cutler," Ben then said.

"Ben Tanner!" Lettice was thoroughly scandalized.

"Well, he's to blame for Plin's trouble. I always figured he was about as straight as a yard of pump water," Ben said obstinately. "I—I found out about him in Portland."

"Then Plin won't have to go back to Boston?"

"How should I know?" Ben growled and lapsed again into gloom.

A horse galloped up to the porch, and a customer entered. Letty swished back to the store.

"Why—why, good morning, Mr. Cutler," Ben heard her stutter.

"What's the trouble, Letty?" a genial voice answered. "You coming down with something?"

Ben jumped to his feet. He started to follow Lettice, changed his mind, and turned toward the back room. He met Amaziah coming out. "He's here," Ben whispered. "He just . . ."

"We saw his horse pass the window," the storekeeper said. "I was expecting him. You and Luther brought in several things he's been waiting for."

He stepped into the store and was greeted with hearty enthusiasm. "Ah—before we look at the new merchandise, there's a matter I'd like to talk over," Amaziah said. "Let's go to the other room."

"So you made it back," Cutler boomed as he followed Amaziah into the kitchen and saw Ben standing there. "Luther must have kept a tight rein on you." He tramped on into the next room, and Ben heard his surprised comment when he found the other two men waiting. Then the door swung firmly shut.

Ben waited. Letty was busy in the store, for a steady procession of chattering women, pigtailed girls, and small boys carrying lists came across the porch. Everyone was eager to see what the trader's wagon had brought.

Letty pressed Ben into service to carry bags of grain to the kitchen door, weigh salt, and measure molasses. Many of the women exchanged knowing looks when they saw Letty's helper. Some of them whispered. One, apparently behind times with the news, asked Letty where Plin had gone. Others took her promptly to one side and told her all about Amaziah's cash box—not without some dispute over the details.

Ben was folding a package with clumsy fingers when he heard the door to the back room open, and boots thumped across the kitchen and down the steps. Ben tapped Lettice on the shoulder and shoved the lopsided package at her. "I have to leave," he muttered. He tore out of the back door and nearly fell against Luther as he skidded down the steps. Horace Cutler's black horse was already galloping up the road.

"It's an unfortunate business," Ben's father declared. "After singing Grimes' praises, it's hard for him to have to admit that his influential friend is a crook."

"Then he *is* the one?" Ben yelped delightedly.

"It seems impossible to deny it," Amaziah agreed. "Cutler had other notes with him, most of them matching the one you were given or the one I'm holding. He didn't seem disposed to argue the matter after a comparison was made."

"Never before saw a man mad enough to pop and having such trouble keeping the cork in." Luther chuckled.

"Apparently his pride wouldn't let him admit the possibility when I talked to him before," Amaziah observed.

"It strikes me," Ben's father said thoughtfully, "that a man so fearful for his own dignity isn't likely to make a fit representative in government. Our state officials have set up new standards for a new state—standards of humility, democracy, and courage."

"They'd likely suffer in Cutler's hands," Amaziah agreed.

"That's one time a calculating man calculated himself right into a corner," Luther said dryly. "Well, I can't stand around here jawing all day—got to get some mowing done or Betsy will be after me with an ax handle."

"Give my apologies to Plin," Amaziah said. "I'll see him personally as soon as I can manage it. Right now, thanks to your wagonload, I've got more business than Lettice can handle alone."

Luther ducked his head by way of reply, grasped his goad, and whistled through his teeth at the blinking team.

Ben watched with a bleak expression as the stocky figure tramped off up the road. He was glad that summer work was pressing and hence his father couldn't spend any more time at the store. They walked home, and Ben went directly to the hayfield, leaving his father to explain the morning's doings to Ma. Will put off mowing as he approached, but when Ben didn't show any sign of talking, he mumbled something about a drink of water and hurried to the house. Ben lifted the scythe out of the apple tree where Will had hung it and tested the edge with his thumb. His broad shoulders swung rhythmically as the hay went down beneath the gleaming blade, and clumps of sweet-smelling clover, stems of buttercups, and cut-off daisies lay in a semi-circle around his feet. Ben took off his shirt, then bent to his work again.

Presently Will and Pa returned. Pa started a swath next to the one Ben was cutting, and Will went back to the shed for the long wooden rake. By dinnertime they had each been twice around the field. Ben had to admit that it was great to put his feet under his own table again. They had beet greens boiled with pork and the custard pie that his mother had promised. Goody chattered and bounced, happy to have him home again.

As he sat that evening, resting his aching muscles against the door frame and watching for the evening star to show above the maples, Ben told them more about the trip: Mother Greene's tall narrow house, the stores and lofts "jammed together so tight you can't see between 'em," and the wonderful things inside the shops. He finished with the tale of the little girl and the lacquer box.

"You've had a grand experience," Ma said softly. "I'm glad for you, and you've made it fun for all of us."

"I don't know. Maybe it would have been better if I hadn't gone at all," Ben said bitterly. "I wouldn't know what I'm missing. Now every time Luther goes, it'll be worse than ever. I just wish I'd never seen that tailor shop. Then I wouldn't have had to mix into Plin's business and maybe . . ." Ben stuck out his chin defiantly. "I wish I'd stayed out of it, anyhow."

"Why, Ben!" his mother said reprovingly. "You know you don't wish any such thing. You wouldn't have been happy traveling with Luther at Plin's expense. I'm proud of what you've done. It takes real courage to speak up in the face of public opinion as you did."

"That's the trouble," Ben said forlornly. "I'll never dare

go to the blacksmith shop again after the men hear what happened."

"Did that bad store man really stab you with his scissors?" Goody asked, her round face puckered with dismay.

"He tried, but all he did was poke a hole in my old moccasins." Ben lifted his feet so that she could see the hole. The heavy new shoes had been put away.

The evening star winked out against the blue-black night sky. "Time to climb the ladder," Ben said.

In the loft, he linked his hands behind his head and stared at the sloping beams of the roof. Will was still down below, reading by the light of his candle. If anybody in the family is brave, it's Will, Ben thought. I'd never have had the nerve to break in and talk up to the men who were questioning Plin. Ben suddenly realized that all of his former ideas were getting turned upside down.

The week passed in a string of back-breaking fifteen-hour days. Bobolinks complained above the heads of the sweating mowers, and bees droned heavily. Goody picked the tiny strawberries that the scythes uncovered, and at meals they were treated to delicious strawberry shortcake.

Ben fitted the hayrack to the oxcart, and the haystack beside the cowshed began to rise, although it had to be rebuilt after Goody and Nancy Cole slid shrieking down its sides one day. As punishment, Goody had to sit on her stool in the corner through all of one golden afternoon and hem a newly woven sheet. Ben knew just how like a prisoner she felt.

He was slumped on the cart tongue that evening, waiting for Will to bring the steers up from the brook, when Luther walked unexpectedly into the yard.

"All tuckered out?" he asked as he shoved back his disreputable black hat.

"Kind of lost interest in work," Ben admitted. He got slowly to his feet.

Luther rocked back on his heels and surveyed the bearskin, now securely nailed to the shed door.

"Pa's out back," Ben said. "You want me to get him?"

"Depends." There seemed to be an undercurrent of humor in Luther's voice. "Seems like you used to pester me to go trading every chance you got. You decided you like haying better?"

"Not so's you'd notice," Ben said.

"Plin's leg is feeling better, and he's got over the shaking-up. I just took him down and got him settled at Amaziah's place. I've released him from any obligation to me."

Ben stared.

"Amaziah rode up to see him a couple of days ago. He allowed he needed a clerk real bad. Letty's set on getting married to Andrew Dole right away. Amaziah said he'd rather have Plin than anyone he knew, so I told Plin to go ahead."

"What did Plin say?"

"Letty sent him a new shirt and Amaziah gave him an inkhorn with his initials on it. Plin looked 'em over and said it'd be too bad not to get some use out of 'em, so he'd take the job."

"That's good," Ben said sincerely.

"I'm not so sure," Luther said, rubbing his whiskers. "That leaves me without any help."

"You wouldn't want . . ." Ben swallowed and tried again. "I mean, if you can't find anyone, I'd . . ."

"I suppose if I took you, I'd be risking my neck," Luther grumbled. "No telling but what I'd end up in jail, traveling with a hothead like you."

"I swear I'd not do anything to get you in trouble!" Ben said, so earnestly that his voice shook.

Luther eyed him keenly. "You reckon you've learned a little respect for other folks' opinions?" he asked sternly. "Can you buckle down and learn trade values and hold yourself in when it comes to violence?"

"Yes, sir!" Ben shouted, elation beginning to shine in his face. "My brother will help me with the ciphering. I've already learned a lot about money . . ." Ben's voice dropped as a thought shook him. "If I go back to Portland, will the sheriff . . . ?"

Luther laughed. "I doubt that Grimes is bringing any charges. Now it looks as though you'd better call your pa so we can clear this deal with him."

At supper, Ben couldn't stop talking. The words tumbled out as he told again of the busy stores in Portland. Trade that crowded the roads and the sea lanes, and kept the looms and forges busy—trade in which he would take part.

"Sounds as though we have a trader in the family," Ben's father observed as the monologue went on and on. "A real Yankee trader."

A child called in the lane, and Goody slipped from the table to see who was coming. "It's Nancy Cole," she called over her shoulder and ran to meet the visitor. A moment later the two little girls skittered into the cabin, followed by Jennett Peck.

"I brought back your shuttle, Mrs. Tanner," she said, smiling. "Nancy's mother also wants me to apologize for Nancy's part in tearing down the haystack."

"Pshaw, that was only a thoughtless prank," Goody's mother said. "How's Phoebe getting along?"

"She's much better. I'll be going home soon, I expect."

"Have a seat here and I'll fix a cup of tea. Ben's been telling us about his trip. He's going with Luther again as soon as the haying's well along."

Ben seemed to have been struck dumb, but managed to nod agreement. Goody and Nancy were in the chimney corner, strumming the jew's-harp and giggling.

"I don't think I have the time for tea," Jennett said. "I must get Nancy home by bedtime. I'd love to hear about Portland some other time, though."

"I shan't let you walk back alone," Ben's mother declared. "One of the boys can go along in case there are any varmints abroad."

"Oh, fiddle," protested Jennett.

Ben scraped back his chair. "I'll go," he said firmly. "I got rid of one nuisance last week, but there might be more."

"I saw the bearskin on the barn," Jennett said as they started off.

"Not much," Ben said offhandedly. "I'm thinking of giving it to Plin. I can always shoot another."

"Do they bother you on the road? It must be dreadful wild in the White Hills?"

"I have more trouble with 'em right here at home," Ben said ruefully, "but if we did meet up with one, I could take care of him."

"Portland must be a wonderful place." Jennett sighed. "I guess all the ladies wear silk gowns and have Turkey carpets on the floors of their houses."

"Don't you believe it," Ben assured her. "The streets are crowded with people, and I saw a lot of fine dresses, but most of the girls wore cloth of their own spinning."

"I'd love to have some gilt buttons for the dress I'm making to wear at Lettice Barber's wedding."

"Why, I'll get you some buttons," Ben promised grandly. "Not in time for the wedding, but the next time I come home."

"Would you truly?" Jennett's blue eyes were wide and admiring.

Ben's heart thumped as though he were running uphill, and here he was only lazing along the road.

The sunset's afterglow tinted the June grass beside the road and the little puffs of dust that followed Nancy's feet as she ran ahead. Ben's thoughts skipped ahead, too, to the wedding. There'd be dancing, and he'd wear his fine new shoes and breeches and his best linen shirt as he danced with Jennett. His spirits soared. And if other people should mention something special that they'd like brought back from the city—buttons and such—he'd make a note to get the things. A trader had to keep his customers in mind all the time.